D1740841

Prove It
TOP SHELF
An imprint of Torquere Press Publishers
PO Box 2545
Round Rock, TX 78680
Copyright 2011 © by Chris Owen
Cover illustration by Alessia Brio
Published with permission
ISBN: 978-1-61040-254-5
www.torquerepress.com

**If you enjoyed Prove It,
you might enjoy these Torquere Press titles:**

Acquired Tastes by Chris Owen

Bareback by Chris Owen

The Broken Road by Sean Michael

By Degrees by JB McDonald

Kegs and Dorms by Jane Davitt, Kiernan Kelly, Tory
Temple, and Stephanie Vaughan

Prove It

Prove It
by Chris Owen

Torquere Press, Inc.

romance for the rest of us

www.torquerepress.com

Prove It

Dedication

To the girls at the NBCCD. Thanks for the giggles, Chris

Author's Note

Dear Reader; In order to keep the flow of the story going, I took occasional liberties with facts in this book, including the academic schedules at Stanford. All errors are happily mine, and I hope you'll overlook them in favor of enjoying the boys' lives.
Chris Owen, 2011

Prove It

Prologue

The first time Silas Cook and Warren Geddis met, they were both five years old and were more or less tossed together in the pit of pre-school daycare.

It didn't go well.

Silas wasn't one to go with the flow or follow directions, which was his mother's primary motivation for putting him in pre-school. Warren was that special kid who would grow up constantly policing his peer group to see who wasn't paying attention or following the rules until the pressure of junior high socialization silenced him.

"It's okay," Silas' mother said to Warren's in a resigned tone. "It's only cheese and yogurt. Imagine the mess they would have made if the snack had been chocolate pudding."

Warren's mother was mortified; Silas' was getting used to it. "I think the phrase 'boys will be boys' is so much garbage," she said thoughtfully. "However, 'Silas will be Silas' seems to be proving true."

From there, Silas and Warren embarked upon a stormy, vocal, and occasionally messy relationship. Their time in first grade was punctuated by long periods of ignoring each other and a short burst of bonding over potty jokes. In the first half of second grade, they were joint masterminds of what became known as the Great Cookie Kidnap Caper, but they promptly had a fight over who got to keep their ill-gotten gains, and then refused to even speak to each other for over two months. By the time third grade came around (the teachers were pulling straws for them, according to unverified rumors), they settled into a prolonged stretch of tolerating one another despite Silas' penchant for disrupting the class and Warren's need for order. They only had two real fights between the ages of six and eight, but those had been horrible enough to give both mothers nightmares.

The evening after the second fight, which took place at the end of third grade, the mothers met by chance in the liquor section of the grocery store, exchanged a long look, and each bought wine. Despite the screaming fit Silas and Warren had engaged in—arguing over a rule in chess—there wasn't animosity between the mothers. They were, however, weary enough from the fallout (lunchtime detentions and a promise from the principal to keep the boys apart for the next grade) that they couldn't even form words for each other.

For Silas, the fourth grade seemed to be less fun. The work wasn't that much harder, the teachers weren't that much more unreasonable about such things as sharing opinions and interesting bits of information he'd picked up from TV and the older boys in the neighborhood, but there was a spark missing.

Warren, on the other hand, gloried in the fourth grade. Everything was quiet and calm, and he could get his work done in class. It was the year of no homework. It was the year he read more than anyone else, and it was the year he won the spelling bee. It was also the year that he decided to be a poet. His back-up plan was also to be a sociologist, but he really hoped that being a poet would suffice.

The summer when they were ten years old, Silas started trying to make money. He didn't have a goal in mind for something to buy; he just knew that he wanted money. People with money had power and friends and cars and apartments of their own, and Silas wanted that. He found after a few days that there was almost no profit in lemonade stands, and he started knocking on doors, asking for chores to do.

Silas' mother was grateful he wasn't asking for money, but gave him a very long lecture about "stranger danger" and how knocking on doors was simply a bad idea.

Stymied, Silas sat on the front lawn for an hour and plotted how to get his hands on a steady source of income.

Warren cruised by on his bike, half a block ahead of his mother.

"Hey!" Silas called, standing up. "Hey, Warren!"

Warren braked but didn't get off his bike. "What?" Deeply suspicious, he watched as Silas came closer to him. Silas wasn't a bully, was in fact a very popular kid, but Warren wasn't terribly comfortable around him. Silas was enthusiastic, and enthusiasm was something to be expressed in moderation.

There was nothing moderate about Silas.

"I want a job. You got any ideas?" Silas was feeling perky and hopeful, his cup brimming full of eagerness and his surety that everyone would be as into his plan as he was.

Warren blinked slowly. "Me?"

"You're the smartest guy I know. Where can I get a job?" It made sense to Silas to ask the smartest guy he knew. Who else would he ask, after all?

Warren thought about it. His mother pulled up next to him and said hello to Silas. She was careful to be cheerful.

Silas said hi back, but he was watching Warren intently. Hopefully.

"Well," Warren said slowly. "You might try the health food store on the corner. They do weird stuff; they might let you do something." Then he pushed on his pedals and headed off down the block, his confused mother going with him.

Silas watched him go and smiled slowly. Brilliant.

On the first day of fifth grade, Silas tracked Warren down in the hallway and presented him with three granola bars, one of which had actual real chocolate in it, instead of carob. "Here. These are for you." He presented them with a grin and a hand flourish that he'd been practicing for three days.

"Huh?" Warren shook his head. He was trying hard to use words and not merely syllabics so he would sound thoughtful instead of thoughtless. "I mean, why? Where did you get them?"

"The health food store!" Silas beamed at him. "You were right, they let me do stuff! But they couldn't give me a paycheck 'cause of the child labor laws or something, so they paid me for sweeping the floor by giving me these!"

Warren took a step back from the force of Silas' glee. "But why are you sharing them with me?" Warren wasn't surprised Silas had gotten what he wanted, but the gift of snack bars was confusing.

"Because you gave me the idea of asking there. This is your cut." Silas was still grinning at him. "Ten percent of my earnings. Thank you!" Silas had been reading up on high finance, and he liked the idea of rewarding the idea men. He turned and walked down the hall, his whole body bouncing with every step.

Warren watched him go, holding the bars, letting other kids jostle him. Silas had deliberately not eaten these bars, had saved them for him on purpose. Silas had thought about him. Warren carefully stowed the bars away in his book bag and decided he'd think about that for a while.

Maybe Silas' enthusiasm had a good side.

By the time they were in junior high, Silas was firmly established as the most popular kid in school. He was confident and sociable, an average student who could have been great if he'd applied himself, athletic and funny. He had a cluster of friends who followed his lead, and while his lead sometimes earned them lunch hours spent cleaning bathrooms or moving books for teachers, they weren't getting into serious trouble. He was fair-haired and tall, a bit on the skinny side, but it was generally assumed that when he stopped having so much energy and slowed down a little, he'd fill out.

Warren, on the other hand, was bookish and solemn, the undisputed academic leader in their grade. He was always first with the correct answer, and always the first one asked to explain things to the other students when a teacher needed another set of hands. If he wasn't reading a book, he was writing in one, and aside from gym class, he was never seen participating in a sport. He was not as tall and skinny as Silas, but to his mother's great relief, he was conventionally handsome and not at all physically awkward. He had a loose-limbed grace and dark hair, and his cheekbones were so sharply defined that he was in danger of being pretty, saved by a square-cut jaw and deeply set eyes. She knew just how miserable his life would be if he was the physical embodiment of every single thing nerdy.

It was bad enough as it was. They'd reached the age where peers were more important than just about anything, and friendships were more about alliances than shared interests or affection. Silas didn't have any trouble gaining alliances or navigating the social waters— though he was starting to have difficulty with his chronic academic underachievement. Warren wasn't precisely friendless, and he wasn't actively disliked at all; he was merely and completely invisible unless he was thrust into the spotlight of student rankings in classrooms. Warren told his mother, when asked, that he didn't care.

For the most part, that was true. He had books, and he had a few people to talk to about the things he read or saw on television or the computer games he played. He wasn't unhappy.

His mother worried.

Silas kept working at the health food store, moving up from sweeping floors to stocking shelves, and he shared his bounty with Warren every two months. He was always so pleased, and even when Warren told him that he didn't have to, that he'd more than paid up for the suggestion, Silas kept doing it.

Silas seemed to really like giving things to Warren.

Silas' mother took many phone calls from giggling girls. She watched her son, completely oblivious to the attention, and began to wonder.

When they were thirteen, Warren discovered *The Lord of the Rings*, Silas discovered he needed a lot of help in math if he was going to avoid summer school, and a boy named Talbot Pelto moved into town and into their class. Tal could draw, and he could draw well. He knew what a hobbit was, and he'd heard of Shakespeare, had even seen a production of *Macbeth* with his parents. He wasn't as bookish as Warren, or quite as suave as Silas (as suave as a thirteen-year old can be), but he held his own in both directions. He had a swimmer's frame, dark blond hair that bleached pale in the summer, and blue eyes that were the talk of the girls in their grade.

Silas invited him for a sleepover within a week, and Tal joined that loose collection of friends.

Warren, his nose deep in *The Two Towers* one lunch hour, wasn't paying attention on his way to his locker. The only warning he got was a yell of "Hey, Bookworm!"

and then his book was gone, thrown down the hallway by a group of laughing kids he only vaguely knew. He blinked, confused, then asked for his book back. What else was there to do, after all?

The potential for a horrible growth experience went up when the group gathered in a ragged half-circle around him and the taunts started.

"Aw, does he need his book?" That was in baby talk.

"Books are paper, Warren. Not friends." Said as if speaking to one exceptionally dumb, which was ironic.

"At least he's got good arms with all that heavy lifting. He's not a complete dork." Someone wasn't sure how to bully, yet.

"But look what he's reading!" Spoken by someone not familiar with novels, clearly.

Warren didn't move. "Where's my book?" he asked calmly. He'd read about this kind of thing, had been waiting for it on some level. As long as they didn't touch him, he'd be okay, at least until he got home after school. "I hope you didn't tear it."

"It's paper," the explainer said, laughing. "Paper tears. It's not like you can't get a new one, Bookworm."

Warren shrugged. "It's a library book. You'll have to replace it."

A snort of derision and the boy took a step forward. Warren was taller. "You think you're so smart."

"Yes, actually." Warren nodded at him. "And I think you're an idiot."

He probably would have been hit, or spat on, or threatened in some more serious way if a hand hadn't come between them, pushing the bully back. "Cut it out, Ricky." Silas was there, rolling his eyes and diffusing the situation merely by walking into it instead of away from it. "There are teachers around the corner, and you know that Warren is smart. There's a book in the library about insults, though." He managed to offer the last as if it were an actual helpful suggestion instead of sarcasm. Maybe it was.

Tal was walking down the hall to get Warren's book, and by the time he'd walked back with it, the crowd had scattered, melting away like ice cubes in the sun, leaving only a few scattered pages from a notebook behind them. Tal liked that they were going so fast, really, since he was still the new kid and too many faces made him feel confused and worried that he'd get names wrong.

"This fell out," he said, handing Warren a slip of paper. "Did you write it?" Tal wasn't big on filters. No question was too personal, but his saving grace was that he never minded if someone told him to buzz off. He liked Warren, though, and hoped that the question wasn't going to make Warren twitchy.

Warren took it and the book, nodding. He didn't trust himself to speak. Anger was welling up, far too late.

"I love poems," Tal said, utterly matter-of-fact. "How about you, Silas?" Warren was turning a shade of pink that Tal didn't like.

"Yup." Silas had read four poems in his life, all for class. "Come on, Warren. There's still hot cookies in the cafeteria." They turned Warren and walked him down the hall, the three of them keeping step on the way to cookies, like they were the Three Musketeers.

They'd eaten two cookies each and were on their way back to the lockers before Warren found his voice. "Thanks," he said, giving each of them a quick glance. "And thanks for getting my book. And the paper."

"No problem," Tal said. He stopped at his locker, the first on their path. "It's a good poem. You got more?" He really did like poems.

Shyly, Warren nodded. No one had ever asked for more, other than his mom.

"Cool." Silas grinned at him. "I'll swing by your place on the way to school tomorrow morning, then we'll grab Tal, okay? You can tell us about them. Or teach me math. Whatever." Silas didn't care which. He was just high on cookies and feeling good. Tal and Warren and him could walk to school together and it would be fun.

Warren rolled his eyes.

Tal grinned. "Or, you know. We can talk about Mario Brothers." Poetry could wait, and math absolutely could wait.

"That."

The three of them smiled at each other, and Warren felt better than he had in ages.

Chapter One

The Great Campout
The summer between eighth and ninth grades, told in three-part disharmony

Summer vacation was only two weeks old when Silas' mother banished him to the garage. She said it was so he could sort out and organize the mess for her, but he was reasonably sure that she'd just had enough of him hanging around the house. He did his hours at the health food store, of course, but he had a lot of free time to fill, and being an only child, he naturally looked to his mom to provide entertainment.

Apparently the TV and video games and music and playing soccer in the house were all too much for her. He protested, loudly, but she remained firm.

"Garage, Silas. You have eight more weeks to get it all figured out. I want to be able to park the car in there during winter, and it's not like we use any of the junk out there, anyway. Just put the broken stuff at the curb and sort out the tools and things. You can do it."

Silas looked at the walls of the double-car garage, piled high with boxes, bins, and random things, and turned to her. "Can I keep the money from the garage sale?"

She rolled her eyes, told him she was going to inspect all the items before he tagged them and sold everything, and said yes.

Within an hour, Silas had his work crew busy moving things and peering in boxes. Warren and Tal didn't have anything else to do, and their moms were just as eager as Mrs. Cook was to have them doing something productive. Tal was more into it than Warren was, but Silas truly didn't mind if Warren took reading breaks. Tal took basketball breaks, and Silas just took breaks. It all had a way of balancing out.

For the first day, they worked more or less at a steady pace, taking the bulk of the real junk to the curb: a shelving unit that was missing support screws and a rear foot; a tent that had a huge hole in it where Silas had made a new door when he was eleven; bent bicycle wheels. There was a load of newspapers that even Silas' mother admitted she'd never get around to throwing in the right bin for recycling, since she and Silas were chronically over the weight limit anyway. Also dumped was a large bag of yarn that smelled funny, and piles of packing material from years of parcels. By the end of the day, Silas' mother was impressed, Warren and Tal were glad the junk part was done, and Silas was counting his coins before he'd earned them.

Days two and three followed along in the same way as the boys sifted through some of the boxes, and Warren took over cleaning the actual tools and putting them on a pegboard they'd found. Tal thought it was an easy job until he saw how meticulous Warren was being about the flakes of rust, then he went back to putting books in piles. Pile one was "looks okay," pile two was "old paperbacks, why did she keep these?" and pile three was "gross and falling apart." The gross ones gradually made their way to the curb.

Silas was going through milk crates, looking for stuff that he could sell for serious money. He wanted to save up at least a hundred dollars over and above the actual cash the health food store was paying him, due to his sudden discovery of a mysterious thing called "fashion." By the end of the third day, though, all he had in the sell box were two table lamps and a full set of plastic picnic dishes. He was starting to think his mother had scammed him pretty good.

"I gotta work tomorrow afternoon," he told Tal and Warren. The three of them were sitting on lawn chairs in the middle of the garage, facing the street. Warren had a broad streak of dirt across his cheek, and Tal's jeans were grimy. Silas was on day three of wearing his favorite Old Navy shirt, and the other two were gradually moving farther away from him.

Mr. McDermott was mowing his lawn across the street and grinning every time he happened to look over at them. He seemed to find them infinitely amusing. One of the times he looked over, he waved; then he went back to mowing his lawn, shaking his head a little as he did.

Tal looked at Warren. "What are you doing tomorrow?"

Warren shrugged, like Silas knew he would. "Maybe helping my mom in the garden. Reading. You know."

Tal nodded and leaned back in his chair so the front legs lifted off the ground. "Yeah. Maybe I'll come over."

"You know," Silas said, trying to make his idea sound appealing, "if you're bored, you guys can come over here and open a few more boxes."

They both snorted at him, but he noted that they didn't tell him to shut up, and they didn't say no. That didn't mean, however, that he was taking it for a yes. Even Silas wasn't that optimistic.

The next day he went to work at the health food store,

content to stock shelves, sweep up the floors, and lug the big vats of all-natural peanut butter up from the cellar. His mind was in the garage and the fortune just waiting to be found in those boxes, so he worked his way through his shift, letting his body do what needed doing while his imagination pondered treasures.

He got home just after five and was halfway up his drive before he realized that Warren and Tal were there, the lawn chairs turned to face the side wall of the garage, the wall that was shared with the house. They were eating beef jerky that his mother must have given them, and they glanced over from whatever they were looking at just long enough to give him a half-wave of welcome.

"Look what we found," Tal said, pointing with his jerky. "Your mom said we could see if it works."

Warren was nodding, his gaze once more aimed at the wall. "It's not too bad."

Silas, his dreams and hopes going so high so fast that he could feel his fingers tingle, almost ran the last few steps into the garage. "What?" he asked, answering his question with a glance. An old floor-model television was wedged in between a golf bag full of clubs that his mother used twice a year and the old air conditioning unit that his mom was going to have to get someone to pick up. On top of the TV were two boxes of VHS tapes and the VCR that Silas remembered from before they got the DVD player. "I wonder how much we can get for it?"

Tal and Warren shrugged in unison. The TV wasn't hooked into the cable, so it was picking up a snowy-looking local channel. They were watching a rerun of some sitcom.

Silas moved closer to take a look at the VHS tapes. There was an assortment of recorded-from-TV tapes, and he'd only started to flip through them when two voices told him to kindly get out of the way so they could watch their show. "You've seen it before," he said, rolling his eyes. He did, however, take the two boxes to his own chair. Aside from the recorded TV (put right into the junk pile), there were a few movies from his childhood that made him smile. The second box was labeled "Liz and Susan."

"Susan is my mom's older sister," Silas said as he opened the box. "She says Mom was always taking her stuff." The box was full of more VHS movies, and most of them seemed to star the same group of people. He read the backs with growing amusement. "You guys have to stay over tonight. We can watch and mock."

Warren snorted. "Mock? Have you been reading a new book? With dialogue and narrative?"

Silas flipped him off, then looked around to make sure his mom didn't see, or Mr. McDermott. "I've been listening to Katie and Grant down at the store. They talk like that all the time."

Tal leaned over and dragged the box of tapes closer to him. "Anything good?"

"Old movies from the Eighties. I wonder how much I can charge for them?"

"Fifty cents apiece." Tal sounded sure. "Maybe a buck for the ones with that red-headed girl in them."

Silas sneered. "What? That's crazy."

"They're VHS, man. Do you still have a VCR in the house? Does your mom have these movies on DVD?"

Tal had a point, Silas had to admit. "Well," he said with a very small sigh, "at least we can watch them and they won't be snowy. Maybe I can get twenty bucks for the TV. When you guys have supper, ask your moms if you can sleep over. We'll close the garage doors and sleep in here!"

They both looked interested in that suggestion, and Silas made a mental note to let his mother know that they'd need to strip the couch of all the cushions. This was going to be great. Popcorn, movies, and his buddies. What could be better? They could start with *The Breakfast Club* and end with... He pulled a tape out of the box. "*Stand By Me*. Ohh, based on a book! Warren, you'll love it."

Warren glanced over and looked away again, like he knew he was being teased but couldn't resist knowing. "Who wrote the book?"

"Stephen King."

"We're watching that one!" Tal bounced out of his lawn chair, which was a feat of dexterity. "I'll be back in an hour. Come on, Warren. Let's get going—faster gone, faster back."

Warren nodded and turned off the TV as he got up. "The VCR works. We didn't want to get into your mom's stuff, but we tested it."

"Cool." Silas grinned at them. "Thanks, guys. See you in a bit, okay? Come back as soon as you can, and bring all the crappy junk food you can carry."

Tal laughed, and he and Warren left, heading down the block to where they'd branch off from each other to go to their own homes. Silas watched them going for a driveway or two, thinking about selling the TV, and then he went in the house to have supper. "Hey, Mom?" he called, toeing off his sneakers at the door. "Me and Warren and Tal are gonna sleep in the garage tonight, okay?"

She was watching TV and making a list of some kind. "Why on earth would you want to do that? Oh, the TV." She looked amused, her mouth quirking into a smile. "No yelling or anything like that. I don't want the neighbors to complain. And keep the volume down."

"Sure!" Silas went to the kitchen to look in the oven. "Roast? Is it done?"

"Ten minutes, it's resting. Go shower, Silas." She didn't sound like the point was up for negotiation.

Silas showered, they ate, and he hauled the camping mattress out to the garage as well as the cushions from the old couch. When his mom started rambling about common sense and the lack of it in teenaged boys, he put a sheet down under them. Honestly, she got wound up about the strangest things. The cushions had two sides, after all. If one side got messy, you could just flip it over.

When Warren and Tal came back, they were armed with their sleeping bags and a shopping bag full of junk food.

"My mom said that if she hears one thing about us being too loud, she's going to ban all sleepovers for the whole summer." Warren was simply stating a fact, as far as Silas could tell. He did that; it was like he couldn't just keep quiet, he had to say what he'd been told, but it didn't really matter to him any more than it did to Silas. Tal was there, after all, and he seemed to have a spooky kind of sense about when the three of them were about to hit a line that an adult would take exception to. They'd learned to listen to him when he said things like "quiet down," or "duck."

Tal nodded and caged the chair that didn't have a missing strip of webbing. "So, what's first?"

Silas rocked up onto the balls of his feet. "*Back to the Future*. And then... *Back to the Future 2!*" He waited until they'd nodded, and Warren had stopped fussing with his sleeping bag on top of the cushions. "Then, later, I want to play that *Stand by Me* one. Stephen King." He tried to wiggle his eyebrows. "When it's late, of course."

"Of course." The sound of a chip bag popping open punctuated the agreement, and officially started the movie fest.

It was several hours later, measured in bags of chips,

trips to the kitchen for pop, trips to the bathroom, one walk around the block to stretch their legs, and a pause while Silas' mother came in to say good night, when the three of them sat in the suddenly dark garage and silence fell. They'd even watched through the credits of *Stand by Me*.

Silas fumbled his way to the light switch and then they were blinking at each other, squinting from the glare of the one bare bulb.

"Holy crap." Silas said. He was almost breathless. "That was… incredible."

Tal was nodding, still in his chair. "Awesome."

Warren got up and stretched. "It was something. I'll need to read the story to see how true they stayed to the text."

That didn't even need a comment. "We are so doing that."

Warren snorted and headed toward the door to the house. "No way."

"Yes way!" Total way. "We might not be twelve going on thirteen anymore, but we're like them! We're at the *cusp*, man. We need to go on an adventure."

"You got a dead body somewhere?" Tal asked. He grinned as he stood up. "I don't wanna die, is all I'm sayin'. No train tracks."

Warren nodded. "That. No bodies, no train tracks." He went into the house, and Silas focused his pitch directly on Tal.

"Camping. You and me and the bookworm. Like, roughing it for real. Trying to live off the land!" It would be glorious. The three of them hiking and exploring and hunting for food, becoming men. Freaking awesome.

Tal pulled off his sneakers and sprawled on his sleeping bag, taking over the camping mattress. "And where, exactly, are you planning to find this wilderness?"

"The city park woods behind your house." It would be perfect.

The unbelievable awfulness of it was beyond belief. There were more bugs than any previous summer of Warren's life, and the unrelenting humidity was making his clothes stick in very awkward places. He'd worn jeans to protect his legs from the undergrowth, and a long-sleeved T-shirt, which had already been torn at the elbow by a branch. His hoodie was tied around his waist, where it was rubbing in a way that boded ill for later in the day. He had the heaviest backpack—mostly because he'd been the only one who knew that "fending for themselves" was totally not going to work, so he'd brought food.

"How far around are we going?" Warren asked Silas. Tal was about ten feet behind them, still trying to trim a branch he'd found down to the right length to serve as a walking stick. He wouldn't stop to do it with the hatchet he'd brought, so it was turning into an all day project with his father's pocket knife. Maybe he wanted to take all day, since the only other thing they were doing was walking.

"To the other side, of course." Silas grinned at him. "We only have about three square miles to wander in, after all. The trees, the hill, the creek. That's it. We'll go to the other side of the wood, then up the hill to find a place to camp."

"What happens when the cops show up in the middle of the night to send us home?" Tal called.

Silas turned and walked backward. "They won't. Why would they? We'll be quiet and everything. It's not like we'll be setting off fireworks. Did your dad call about campfires?"

Tal nodded and sliced a sliver of wood off his stick. "Yeah, the fire index is okay. He was asking about burning brush, and they said not within city limits, but those metal fire pit things are okay."

"We don't have a fire pit thing," Warren pointed out. He got identical looks of exasperation in return.

"That is why," Silas said in that tone he used when he was explaining the obvious, "we will dig a deep pit, line it with rocks, keep the fire very small, and have a jug of water right next to it." He pointed over his shoulder at the empty jug strapped to his backpack. "We'll fill it in the creek, later on."

Warren rolled his eyes but said nothing. He was pretty sure that a fire on a hill in the middle of the town would have someone out taking a look.

"Do you think we'll be able to see all the way to Birchline?" Tal smacked at a mosquito, thankfully not using the hand holding the knife.

"Why? Who lives in Birchline?" Birchline was a subdivision not far from where they all lived on the West Flat. Silas was walking forward again, his jeans making scraping sounds on the pokey branches of the undergrowth. "Ow." He didn't have a long-sleeved shirt on.

"Lindsay." Tal used a tone so casual it was completely fake, and Warren saw Silas surreptitiously lift one finger for Warren to see. Warren shook his head. That totally didn't count; Silas had practically invited Tal to talk about a girl. Silas made a face but dropped the finger.

"You can send her smoke signals later," Warren said. "Although she probably won't know what they say. Not a lot of girls do."

Silas and Tal both laughed, Silas at the joke and Tal apparently at Warren. "You're an expert on girls now? What book did you read about them?"

"And can Tal borrow it?" Silas grinned at them both. "He needs all the help he can get."

"Oh, shut up." Tal threw a handful of leaves at Silas. "Like you'd know. Both of you."

Warren let them argue back and forth about who was more lame—the guy who was gaga for girls or the guy who hadn't really paid attention to the fact that they existed—and pondered the concept as they walked. He was, of course, perfectly aware that *he* was a late bloomer. He'd read hundreds of books, maybe thousands, and they all seemed geared to point out a few facts of life that Warren had yet to see proven true in his own life. The Good Guys Always Win was one that he was always watching for. The boys and girls thing seemed a lot more important to other people, and there was the whole "some boys like boys" thing, which Warren had given thought to. He was okay with the concept, but uninterested in that, either. Classic late bloomer.

Silas, on the other hand, had embraced all the typical teen things right on schedule, dragging Warren and Tal along with him. There had been sports and movies, junk food and staying up too late playing video games, and casual cussing. He'd been the leader of their pack development by sheer pushiness until Tal's interest in girls had washed over the three of them, amusing Silas and making Warren roll his eyes with increasing frequency.

Warren took it as a matter of course, but for the first time since Warren had met him, Silas seemed unsure how to react. He ignored Tal's new obsession for a while, then got rude about it for a day or two. He stopped when Tal gave him a look of genuine hurt and confusion. Silas may have been impulsive and occasionally unaware of how he swept Warren and Tal along, but at heart he was a good person and not one to cause injury if he could help it. He stopped being mean about Tal's fascination with girls' hair and how they smelled, and he didn't even make gagging noises when Tal talked about kissing, but he did find an outlet for his confusion-disguised-as-amusement: he started betting with Warren.

They weren't exactly up for high-stakes betting, since Silas was still only working at the health food store and Warren's only sources of income were his mother and mowing lawns for the neighbors on either side of his house. Silas was still trying to accumulate as much personal wealth as he could, for reasons he probably hadn't worked out yet, but Warren was happy enough to play for bragging rights. The current bet, always managed as discreetly as they could, was about the number of times Tal would mention the current girl holding his interest over the weekend. Warren was sure that Tal would keep it to under fifty; Silas was angling for seventy-five.

"Hey, Warren. Still with us?" Silas slapped Warren on the arm as he strode past. "Not about to die of the bugs?"

Warren scratched a new bite on his neck, suddenly aware of each itch he had. "We should have brought spray." He didn't want to tell them, didn't want to appear to be a wimp, but Warren had bug spray in his backpack, along with the food and more water and a change of clothes. He had two books as well, and a flashlight, and there was a thick blanket crammed down at the bottom. His back was sweating so much from the bag that he was sure his shirt was soaked right through, and the waistband of his jeans, which had been only threatening to rub his skin raw, suddenly seemed to be on the edge of making him bleed. "Tell me again why we're walking all the way around the park to the other side, off the trails, instead of just going right up the hill from our side?"

Silas gave him a hard look and sped up, almost marching as he led the way through the underbrush.

"Because," Tal said patiently, coming up to walk

beside Warren, "we are grand adventurers, coming of age in the wilds of the downtown rural atmosphere."

"And that means we can't take the paths?"

"That means we can't take the paths. Or use the public restroom."

Warren made a face. At least it wasn't raining. "Hey, did anyone check the forecast for tonight?"

"Yes, Warren." Silas spoke with exaggerated care, dragging each word out. "It will be fine, I promise. No one will kill us. No one will come and tell us to put out the fire. No one will get rained on. It'll be perfect."

Tal rolled his eyes. "You just jinxed us, man. Thanks a lot."

Warren sighed, reseated his backpack, and marched on, hoping that it would be cooler by the creek, and warm overnight. He took comfort in there being no train tracks, no dead bodies, and no sense of fear or despair pushing them on. Just Silas, leading them on like the Pied Piper, and the relentless chatter of Tal going on about Lindsay's boobs. Silas was keeping track of how many times her name came up, Warren was sure.

"Do you hear that?" Silas stopped walking and Tal broke off his oration, both of them cocking their heads like puppies.

"It's *traffic*." Warren's mood was having a difficult time standing up to the heat and discomfort. "Can we just get to where we're going to camp?" He slapped a mosquito and splattered blood all over his hand.

Silas glared at him. "Can you just attempt to get into the feel of this, dude? Just a little? Stop being such a stick in the mud."

Warren took a breath, ready to snap back, but Tal swept his hand between them. "Yoohoo, Yahoos. How about we do both? Head right up, ditch the bags, and then spend a couple hours exploring without carrying everything with us?"

Warren and Silas continued to stare at each other. Warren was tired of always backing down and his skin was feeling gross. But then Silas' face cleared, and he grinned as he took one step back. "All right, Tal." He nodded. "Compromise."

Keeping another sigh inside, Warren followed the pair of them, their trajectory changing slightly as they started to climb up instead of swinging around the park. He was just as pleased to do as Tal suggested, but he resented the easy way Silas had of just changing his mind and being completely okay with it. He so rarely made a wrong choice that it left Warren envious of Silas' instincts. Warren's instincts crapped out after anything other than "Will I like this book?" He barely remembered to eat on time if he was involved in something. And there was Silas, marching through life like he was completely comfortable in the world.

Maybe he was.

Maybe Tal was, too, and it was only Warren who was so often out of step.

"Warren. Come on."

Blinking, Warren looked up. They were standing side by side ahead of him, a little above him on the slope. Sun was streaking across the top of Tal's head through the leaves, and they were both looking at him. "I'm coming."

"Good." Tal nodded. "We're waiting for you."

Silas nodded, too, and held out a hand to pull Warren up and over a log.

Warren didn't need the help, but he took the hand anyway, suddenly slightly more in step with the world.

Tal leaned back on his rolled-up sleeping bag, which was propped against a tree, and watched Warren and Silas plan the fire pit. The whole idea of "dig a hole, line it with rocks, and have water handy" was holding firm, but both Silas and Warren were the type to refine an idea to ridiculous degree. It was okay, though, since they both had a great time doing that kind of thing, and they'd just call Tal in when the plan was final and they needed an extra body for labor.

The three of them had spent the day wandering around in the woods, talking about all kinds of things. Warren knew a lot about trees and what kind of wood was good for various things, and Silas, oddly, knew about birds. They all talked about school things for a while—Tal's growing interest in drama club, and Warren's desire to fill out all the blanks possible on a college application. It was amazing how many groups a person could be active in if they really tried, and since Warren was a hard worker, he was planning to be in about seven things. Silas was going to make himself well-rounded by having a job, one sport, one academic club, and one social activity. He hadn't yet figured out any of the details.

"Ten inches would be okay," Warren was saying. "But a foot and a half would be better."

"There's plenty of moisture in the ground, though," Silas argued. "How about a foot and a bit?"

Tal closed his eyes and soaked up the sun. The bugs had gone on to prey upon other creatures, and he was comfortable. He wished they had cold soda with them, but Warren had brought drinking water so that was okay. "When are we going to eat?" he asked.

"Depends what we're eating. If you want hot, we need to get the fire going." Warren was lining up the rocks they'd gathered to line the pit with. "If you just want crackers and chips and nuts and stuff, we can eat any time."

"I brought granola bars," Silas put in, using a trowel to start the hole. "And oranges."

Tal had a jar of peanut butter and three spoons. They were all set. "I'm pretty sure that house was Lindsay's." He'd been real careful when he counted roofs. Too bad she hadn't been out in the backyard or something. There was a brief whispered argument that Tal ignored. "It'd be cool to go back to the lookout spot after dark and see the town lights, you think?"

"Are we going to try to see in her room?" Silas asked with deep suspicion in his voice. Warren smacked him. Tal ignored him.

Later, after they'd gotten the pit dug and ready and eaten a lot of food, they set out into the woods armed only with their flashlights and the knife they'd used to cut kindling. It was amazing how creepy their own tiny woods were in the dark. It was also amazing how many times they could trip over sticks, roots, rocks, and each other. It didn't help that they all jumped at loud noises and there seemed to be some kind of wildlife block party going on.

"Raccoon, not bear," Silas whispered at one point, and that set them all laughing so hard that Tal tripped again. He reached out for a tree to catch himself, but it was Warren and down they tumbled. It wouldn't have been so bad, aside from the dirt and the leaves stuck to them, except they broke one of the flashlights and then he and Silas had to share because Warren got into a snit. Something about his back being sore from carrying all the food.

They got to the lookout, and just as Tal had expected, they could see lights for the whole area. It was like the sky had spilled the stars onto the ground, but he hesitated to say so; poetry was more a Tal-and-Warren thing than a Tal-and-Warren-and-Silas thing.

"Stars," Warren whispered, though, just loud enough for Tal to hear and Silas to miss.

Tal nodded. "Uh-huh."

A few minutes later, he pointed out what he believed to be Lindsay's house, ignored the way Silas punched Warren in the arm, and led them back up to the top of the hill to light their fire.

Which of course didn't want to stay lit at all, and when they ran out of matches, the three of them packed up and went to sleep in the tent that they'd pitched in Tal's backyard.

At least they hadn't come across any dead bodies.

Chapter Two

The Play is The Thing
(Except when it's not)

Warren took advantage of the director's need to talk to Madison, the star of the high school play, and took a break. He sat down in the seat nearest to the stage so he could keep an eye on things, and tried to recall what he'd need for the next scene without checking his notes.

"Are you testing yourself again?" Tal tumbled into the seat next to Warren, his legs appearing to flail as his butt made contact. He'd grown yet again and was having trouble keeping his limbs under control, as everyone who came near him could attest. Warren had been tripped twice the last month, and Silas once.

"No," Warren lied. "I'm good. What are you doing here? I thought you were backstage." Tal was in the play, a small part, but with real lines and even a little character development if the audience squinted the right way.

"Wardrobe has cramps." Tal waved his hand in a way that he'd previously assured Warren was dramatic. "So things back there are a mess. Girls, man. They get shrill when they're in groups like that." He pulled a tube of rolled-up paper out of his back pocket and smoothed it out on his knee. "What do you think? Did I get it?"

What Warren had assumed to be Tal's script was instead a pencil and ink drawing of the auditorium and stage during rehearsals. He took the drawing and looked at it with a critical eye; Tal would pester him relentlessly if Warren wasn't paying close attention and being honest.

The drawing had excellent perspective, something Tal had been working on for more than a year. He'd shown the stage, its angle to the audience from stage right, and the first several rows of seats. The director, Mr. Howell, was in the front row and Silas was in the row behind, apparently either fixing something in his hand or being entirely inappropriate. On the stage were the three leads, and around them Warren could see the controlled chaos of stagehands, other actors, and the chorus, everyone milling around. Someone was sitting at the upright piano, too.

"It's very good," Warren said, meaning it. "I like that you managed to show how bizarre Lillian's hair is without being crazy about it. It's too bad that you can't really show sound, though. I think you have to live in this to really get it."

Tal snorted and took the picture back, jotting in two musical notes over the piano, making them slightly wobbly and discordant, implying that the piano was out of tune. "There."

"Hey, hey, what's this?" Silas leaned between the two of them from the row behind, grinning. "Hi, Tal. Nice to see you got out from backstage."

Warren glanced at the stage to make sure Mr. Howell was still there, talking to Madison. "How come you're not backstage yourself?" Silas had uncharacteristically opted not to audition for the lead role in the play, and instead was the head stagehand, in charge of most everything from sets to marks to lights. He'd roped Warren in as the prop master.

"Same reason you're not—The Man is busy, we're sitting long enough to catch our breath." Silas looked at his watch and then showed it to them both by thrusting his arm out between them. "And we have another hour to go. At least."

"At least." Warren sighed. Being in charge of the props meant he had a lot of cleaning and organizing to do after the rehearsal, since if he didn't know where a prop was, no one would know where it was.

"Assuming Wardrobe gets over the cramps." Tal smirked and worked on his picture.

Warren watched a few girls from the chorus cross the stage and sit by the piano, his gaze tracking them to make sure they didn't mess up the set. He was sure that a few of them deliberately moved goblets and plates around, but when he suggested they glue them right to the table, Silas had refused.

"It's not like they actually need to do fittings right now anyway," Silas was saying to Tal. "They know where to find everyone; ten minutes at lunch would do it."

"Times twenty," Warren pointed out. "That's fine for Tal's lunch break, but they'd be working all the time."

"Oh, right." Silas didn't seem either surprised or bothered. "I guess that could be a problem."

"Yeah, probably." Warren rolled his eyes and then sat up straight as Mr. Howell backed away from Madison. "Back to work, I think."

But instead Mr. Howell moved to the piano to talk to the chorus, and Madison crossed the stage to huddle with her best friend, Sherilynn.

"We'll be here all night at this rate." Warren fell back in his chair, jamming against Silas' hand. "Hey!"

"Sorry." Silas adjusted his position. "So, I think I've

got my mom talked around to letting me get that new game I was telling you about, with the..." His voice trailed off, and Warren turned his head to see why. Then he nudged Tal.

Silas was watching a young man walk past them and up the steps of the stage. "Who is that?" he asked, his head tilting slightly to the side. "I don't recognize him."

Warren shrugged. "Someone's brother?" The guy had on a college hoodie, and there were car keys dangling loosely from his fingers. "Does it matter?"

"Apparently," Tal murmured. He lifted his chin at Silas, and Warren turned around in his seat to look.

Silas was staring as the newcomer crossed the stage. Sherilynn broke away from Madison to talk to him, apparently protesting his presence. Warren wouldn't say that Silas' eyes were bugging out, exactly, but his mouth was literally slack-jawed and he was watching intently. Then he blinked rapidly, three times and once more, and his face lost all color. He went white in an instant, so fast that Warren was alarmed into reaching for him, but then Silas' eyes narrowed and the color came back to stain his cheeks red. Silas nodded sharply, apparently to himself, and stood up. "So. All right, then."

Sherilynn went back to Madison and the young man came down the steps, pausing at the bottom to scan the rows of seats. He blinked and rocked back a little when he spotted the three of them, or maybe it was just Silas. Then he smiled and went to sit at the other end of the front row.

"What the hell?" Warren stopped talking, his own jaw going slack as Silas marched past him, all the way down the row, and took the seat right next to the stranger. Within seconds they were shaking hands and smiling at each other, chatting away with no apparent awkwardness.

"Well," Tal said slowly. "That was interesting. If only

it worked that way with girls."

Warren stared at him.

"Look." Tal lifted his chin again, this time toward the piano. The girl in the middle of the group was looking at them. As soon as she saw them looking back, her eyes dropped and she giggled at the girl next to her. "That's Gabrielle Verner. She's hot."

Warren looked at Gabrielle. She was smallish and blonde and had darkly lined eyes. She appeared to be clean, and her hair was shiny. "I guess." Warren looked down the row to where Silas was talking with his hands and the guy was laughing, clearly charmed.

"And yet," Tal said, "I can't just go up there and talk to her. She's got a posse, for one."

"And you've got a girlfriend, for two."

"There is that." Tal grinned at him. "Or whatever we are. I haven't seen her in a couple of days."

The posse at the piano broke up, and two of them headed to the director. Gabrielle, however, was on a direct path to Tal and Warren.

Tal sat up straight and became intensely interested in a speck of dust on his shoe. Warren snuck another look down the row to see Silas on his feet and the guy smiling up at him, nodding at something Silas was saying.

"Hi, Tally." She giggled and walked right past them. "Warren." She pronounced it "worn."

"Hi, Gabrielle." Tal looked up and smiled at her, watching as she walked all the way around to the stage left stairs and back up to meet her friends.

"I have to go." Warren stood up, his notes clutched tightly in his hand. "Tell..." He had to think and try to order his thoughts, prioritizing his words and putting a sentence in order. "Tell Mr. Howell that I had to go home, but I'll come in tomorrow morning before school to clean up and make sure the props are done."

Tal was looking up at him, his lips pursed. "And what do I tell Silas?"

"Nothing to tell." There wasn't. "Tell him to call me after supper. Or you guys come over. Whatever." He nodded. "Come over after supper. We have to get through that history stuff. Okay?"

"Okay." Tal gave him a long look. "Are you okay?"

"I'm fine." He was about to fly apart. "I'm just done for the day. See you later." Warren turned before Tal could get him talking and left, not looking back. He went up the aisle and out of the auditorium, the sudden near-silence of the hallway thick in his ears. It suited his growing numbness, and he went to his locker, packed up his homework, then left, heading directly home. He tried very hard not to think about anything at all, least of all Silas and what he'd just done.

It didn't work.

By the time he reached his house ten minutes later, Warren was ready to have a nice little private freak-out in the confines of his bedroom, but it was not to be. His mother's car was in the drive and she was right there in the living room, folding laundry while she watched television.

"Hi, honey." She smiled at him and folded a towel. "You're home early."

"Yeah, it... Uh, yeah. I left a little early. They didn't need me, and I have homework." He put his backpack on the floor and headed past her to the kitchen, forgoing the usual chat they had as he unpacked his bag and put things away.

"Whoa. Back it up." She had one hand out, palm facing him. "What's wrong? What happened?"

"Nothing." He went to the fridge and leaned into it, hanging onto the open door. "I don't want to talk about it."

There was a long silence behind him, and he didn't come out of the fridge until his mom said, "All right. I'll be in the living room if you change your mind." She didn't sound anything other than concerned, which was just like her. She wouldn't even get upset at him being short with her if it was because he was upset.

Warren got out the orange juice and filled a glass, drank it all, and filled it again. He walked all the way around the kitchen, the trip taking far less time than it did when he was younger; Tal wasn't the only one growing. He did a second circuit, drank the juice, and put the glass down on the counter too hard. The bang reverberated up his arm, and by the time it reached his shoulder, he was aware that his face was tight, every muscle contracted and aching.

Unable to find a better alternative, since his best friend was the issue and therefore not eligible for being a listening ear, he marched into the living room. His mother muted the TV and kept folding socks. Patient.

"I can't talk to you about this. But I have to, since I need to."

She nodded. "Okay. Will it help if I just listen and don't offer advice of any kind?"

He considered that. "And you have to swear to God that you won't phone anyone. This is very, very private."

"If it has to do with drugs, guns, or stealing, I can't promise that." That was a standard refrain and one that Warren had always taken comfort in. "But anything else, you have my word."

Warren swallowed and nodded. "Okay. Because it's... well, he should find his way on his own, and he sure doesn't need anyone calling his mom."

Her eyebrows went up. "What did Silas do now?"

Warren felt his eye twitch. "Silas is gay."

"Oh." Her eyebrows stayed up. "I see. He told you?"

Her gaze was flicking madly and he had a strong feeling of being inspected for harm. "He didn't... Um. Did he express feelings—"

"Mom! God!" That thought shoved out all the others. "He's my best friend! That's all!"

"Okay, stop yelling. Jeepers." Her cheeks were pink. "It's just you seem so upset that I thought it must have—"

"He just does everything so easily!" It felt like a dam was bursting somewhere inside him and words kept coming, so fast he had to wave a hand to make the air smooth out in his lungs. It was a trick from when he was very little and his mind was so fast that it would race ahead of his mouth and he'd stumble on words all the time. He hadn't had to do it for years. "He just, half an hour ago, looked up and saw a guy, and right before my eyes, right there in front of me, he realized he was gay, dealt with it, and got up and went over and just started talking to this guy. Like, in less than a minute he found out, got over himself, and went and got himself his first boyfriend. How is that right? No drama, no flip out, just... BAM." Warren's eyes stung with sudden tears.

"Oh, honey." His mother looked at him with eyes that were too full of sympathy. "I'm sure he's going to have a freak-out as soon as he gets home and has time to really think."

"Even if he does, it's just so... Silas." Warren wiped his eyes, hating that they were damp. "How does he do it? Mom, he's always been this way, the Golden Child. Everything Silas has tried or wanted has been fantastic, always. I don't get how he can just do things and be okay, every time."

She nodded and looked like she wanted to hug him. "I know, honey. I do. Silas is charmed. But you need to remember, he's your friend, not just because you like him but because he likes you back. You're one of those things he picked and is good at. He gets you like no one else, not even Tal."

Warren shook his head. "I'm not ready to hear good Silas things yet, Mom."

"Okay." She nodded again. "He's going to need your help when he does freak out. Even for Silas, this is a big thing."

"Yeah." Warren sighed and picked up his bag. "I'm going to go do my homework in my room."

"Warren?"

He paused, his back to her, and waited.

"I think that you being freaked out over his reaction and not that he's gay is something wonderful. I'm proud of you."

Warren nodded. "It is what it is. Nothing special." It couldn't be special, even if it was Silas. Not when Warren had been re-examining his own late-bloomer status with increasing frequency.

He went to his room and quietly shut the door, then lay on his bed and lost himself in music and his ceiling until his mom called him to supper.

Chapter Three

Fumbling Toward Ecstasy, Take One

Warren was back in his room when Silas and Tal arrived at seven-thirty, both with their homework and Tal with a huge bottle of water. Tal had decided the previous week that he was dehydrated, and to counter that he was carrying water with him everywhere he went, sipping frequently. Warren and Silas made a game of using the water fountains whenever they passed one, but never spelled out with words that they weren't carrying an awkward and heavy bottle. Warren assumed Tal got the point anyway, but he stubbornly continued to carry his water.

Even though he couldn't concentrate, Warren was sitting at his desk, his history notes out and his pen in hand when they arrived. He didn't get up, but swung around in his chair to watch as Tal sat on the floor and leaned against the side of the bed and Silas dumped his book and notes onto a pillow.

"Was Mr. Howell pissed that I left?"

Tal shook his head. "Nah, I told him you had a headache. But you have to go in early tomorrow to go over things and make sure you know where stuff is."

Warren nodded. "Yeah, I was going to." He looked at Silas. "Are you okay?"

"Sure. Of course. Yes. Why wouldn't I be?" He cleared his throat. "I'm fine. Are you?"

"Yeah, I'm good." Warren and Silas looked at each other and Tal rolled his eyes. "History?"

"History." Silas nodded, threw himself onto the bed, and grabbed his text. "Civil War. Good times."

Tal snorted and opened his own book. "I dare you to say that in your homework."

"Nowhere to put it." Silas pulled out his homework from among his papers, a large timeline they were to have filled in, covering the events of 1861 and 1862. "I suppose it could be a subtitle."

"I wouldn't recommend it," Warren said in a perfect imitation of their history teacher's voice.

Tal laughed and Silas smiled, and Warren looked at his mostly complete timeline. "These are going to get harder, right?"

Silas gave him a withering look. "Got a pencil?"

Warren gave him one from the cup on his desk. "There are still three years left to chart out, and that's even before we hit midterms."

"You're just a ray of sunshine and a bucket of rainbows, aren't you?" Tal said acidly, then he darted a glance at Silas, his eyes wide.

Warren groaned and Silas' cheeks went pink.

"Sorry," Tal mumbled. "I didn't mean... Well. You know what I didn't mean."

"I don't think I'm ready to start flying a flag," Silas blurted, his voice a little too loud. He glanced back at the closed bedroom door. "I just. I think I." He stopped, his cheeks bright with red splotches. "I never thought about it, you know. And then I did. I saw him and I just thought. Yeah." He nodded once and then he looked at his hands.

"It just. Happened."

Warren stared at Silas. His mother had said—and, if he was totally honest with himself, he had known himself—that Silas would have a freak-out. But in Warren's mind, Silas' freak-outs were a lot more emphatic, focused, and articulate. This version of Silas dealing with something was new and unsettling.

Not quite as unsettling as Silas going right up to a guy and chatting him up, but unsettling.

"How did you know he—" Warren closed his mouth with a snap. He shouldn't ask that, not yet.

"I didn't." Silas was still looking at his hands, his cheeks still flushed. "It's not like I walked up to him and asked if I could kiss him, for God's sake."

Tal tilted his head. "Some girls don't mind that."

"Shut up," Warren and Silas both said, without heat. Warren added, "They do, too, anyway. Try it and find out."

Tal huffed but let it go. "What did you say to him, then?"

Warren would have preferred to ask other questions, since wasn't this all about how Silas *knew* and how he felt, after all? But Silas was already answering, his skin returning to a normal color by degrees.

"I just said hi and that I was the stage manager. Was there anything I could help him find? And he said no, he'd already found his sister, but she wasn't ready to leave yet, so he was going to stick around. Then I sat down next to him and told him my name and I kept on talking. He laughed a lot—I don't think it was at me, though."

"I think you'd know," Warren told him. "What's his name?"

"Dillon. He's Sherilynn's brother, and he goes to college. And he works at a nursing home, doing clean up and stuff and talking to the residents. That's nice, huh?"

Silas looked at Warren, his eyes hopeful. "Yeah?"

"Sure, that's nice." Warren shrugged a shoulder. "Talking to the elderly is good."

"Is he into you?" Tal asked bluntly. "'Cause you're only a junior, remember."

Warren glared at Tal. "And you wouldn't date a college girl?"

Tal's eyes went out of focus for a moment and he grinned. Warren rolled his eyes.

"He gave me his number," Silas said, barely above a whisper. "And we're going to meet for a cup of coffee on the weekend."

"You don't drink coffee," Warren pointed out before he could stop himself. He quickly added, "But you can have a fruit smoothie, for sure."

Silas nodded, his gaze darting around the room. "Anyway, so that's that. I did what felt right at the time. Now I feel a little sick, honestly."

Tal and Warren exchanged a look. "How come?" Tal asked carefully. "I mean, it's okay to be gay, man. You know that, right?"

Silas rolled his eyes. "Sure. It just means everything's changed, is all. It'll be fine, but right now it's weird. I honestly never thought about guys at all, was just kind of waiting for the girl thing to kick in and doing my doing. And then, bam. Lightning bolt to the balls, and it's a frat boy."

Warren swallowed nine more questions and scratched his eyebrows. "Um. So, like, when you..." He made a universal gesture understood by all teenage boys. "What do you think about, if it's not girls or guys?" He felt his face heat up. "Never mind."

Tal laughed, a full belly laugh. "And Warren finally admits he's normal and steps out into the real world with us. Welcome to the world of hormones, Warren.

Although, you know. Kind of a personal question."

"I said never mind." Warren wished he'd swallowed that question, even as part of his mind protested that it was totally legitimate. After all, he knew what he thought about, and he was a late bloomer. Silas was his best friend, they'd known each other for two-thirds of their lives, and Silas was newly gay. Warren needed as much information as he could get.

"Mostly just feelings," Silas said thoughtfully. "You know, no person in particular, just what feels good."

A short silence followed that, and then Tal picked up his notes. "So, 1861, huh? Not good times."

"No, not good times." Silas sighed, and the three of them got to work, filling in timelines and listening as Warren hit the highlights for them with a bit more detail. It was a study method that worked well for all three of them.

An hour and a half later, Tal headed home, his water bottle empty, his timeline full, and his eyes looking gritty. "I don't know, maybe I'm coming down with something."

"Cramps?" Warren suggested.

"You're a funny guy." Tal waved at them both and headed out, but came back a moment later. "Oh, I forgot to tell you—the dollar theater is showing *Dr. No* on Saturday afternoon. Want to go?" He was looking at Warren, not Silas. The dollar-theater showings of old classics weren't something Silas had managed to sustain an interest in, but Warren and Tal went as often as they could.

"I'll bring the popcorn," Warren agreed. "See you tomorrow."

"Later, guys." Tal waved again and left.

Warren looked at Silas, still sprawled on his bed. "You might be off having coffee, anyway, huh?"

Silas nodded and sat up, making room for Warren. "I

guess so," he said quietly. "Are you upset with me?"

"No." Warren sighed and sat down on the edge of the bed. "I was never mad at you about it, Silas. I don't care if you're gay—in fact, I'm pretty sure I'm happy that you've figured it out. Now you know and you can go about meeting someone special, or at least figuring out what you want with your life, you know? But I was really..." He searched for a way to explain that was both gentle and honest. "I'm really jealous of how you do things. You saw what you wanted, even though you hadn't ever wanted it before, and then you just went and got it. I couldn't do that in a million years."

"Sure you could," Silas told him, apparently meaning it. "You're a really smart guy; you can get whatever you set out to get."

Warren smiled, knowing that Silas truly thought that. "Well. I don't know what I want yet, so I guess I don't have to worry about it."

Silas gave him a sympathetic look. "Maybe most people don't, you know. I mean, sure, some guys are like Tal and get into the whole girls and dating and wanting to make out a lot thing pretty early. But most people are too confused with just learning math to get there. Maybe."

Though he doubted that, Warren nodded. "So, what was it? That you noticed today that you hadn't noticed before. What is it about Dillon that rang your bell so hard?"

Silas actually blushed. "It's lame."

"Nothing is lame." Warren looked at him. "Something special happened to you today, Silas. You learned something very important about yourself, and nothing about that is lame."

"God, you sound like an after-school special. Or my mother." But Silas looked reassured anyway.

"Did you tell her?"

"Hell, no. I'll tell her some other time. I want to actually have this date, if that's what it is, first."

Warren glanced at him sharply. "You don't know?"

"I think I know. He said I was cute and that he liked my energy."

"It's a date."

"Uh-huh." Silas looked a little smug. "He said he was surprised I wasn't in the show, since I've got the personality for theater."

Warren made a heroic effort not to gag or mock. "He's right," he said instead. "You'd be great at acting. Are you going to tell me what you noticed?"

Silas rolled his eyes and groaned. "Okay, okay. Remember when he walked past us? One of the lights was shining too far upstage and caught the keys in his hand—that's why I looked at him, the flash of light. Anyway, I looked up and there he was, backlit and kind of glowing. And all I could see was this perfect body, all strong and lean. I wanted to touch him, and then I wanted to..." He looked away and rubbed his face. "I wanted to touch him and kiss him and just *have* him. Just like that. Which, you know, isn't something that happens all the time."

"Unless it's Tal and cheerleaders."

"True. But there it was." Silas sighed. "I shouldn't have gone right over to him, I should have gone home to think and take a shower. But I didn't."

"Do you still want to touch him?"

"God, yes," Silas said fervently. "I want to kiss him and feel him and rub up on—"

"Okay, thank you. That's enough." Warren held out a hand, palm showing. "No boob talk from Tal, no dick talk from you. I have rules."

Silas blushed. "Okay. Sorry."

"It's a new rule." Warren waved his hand. "I hope he's nice." He nodded to himself. "I hope he's nice to you, and that you have a good date this weekend."

Silas smiled at him. "Thanks."

"You can tell me about it. Just mind the rules." Warren got up and started cleaning up his notes.

"Deal." Silas got up and gathered his things. "See you tomorrow. I'll go to school early and help you with the props."

"Thanks. Cool." Warren watched him get packed up and walked him to the door. "I'll come by for you."

Silas nodded and left, and Warren turned around to see his mom standing in the kitchen, watching him. "Homework's done," he told her.

"That's nice, dear. How's Silas?"

"Pretty good. Smitten. Coping."

She nodded, then tilted her head at him. "And you?"

"Coping. Not smitten. I'll be okay." He went to the fridge and got an apple, then kissed her cheek. "Thanks. I'm going to bed now."

"All right. I love you, Warren. And I'm proud of you."

"Love you, too, Mom." He went down the hall to his room, wondering what, exactly, a perfect body would look like to him.

Chapter Four

Two Weeks to the Final Summer of Youth

W arren took the problem to the one person he knew would have the absolute correct answer, the one person not seeing the situation through the mist of teenage politics.

"Well, if you're paired up, then I really think you should buy her a corsage. It would be kind, if nothing else." His mother ate one of the slices of mushroom she was adding to a sauce. She was still dressed for the office, though her hair had slipped from most of the clips. "It's very hard on young girls to feel out of place, especially at senior prom. Is she your date?"

Warren, sitting on a stool at the kitchen island so he could steal cut-up vegetables as well, shook his head. "No, not really. I mean, there's a whole group of us going as a unit to avoid having dates. Silas has a date, of course, but Tal said we'd be subversive and have a group date." Warren had figured it would land ass over head, and it had. Teenagers weren't meant to be subversive about the important things like dates and proms. They were meant to talk a good talk and then buy corsages and try to get laid.

He didn't mention the last thought to his mother.

"So... if there's a group of you, why did this even come up?" That was exactly why he was asking her—she'd seen his point immediately. "Who all is going on this group date of yours? Which, by the way, I won't be telling your relatives about."

"Me and Tal and Silas, of course," he started, ticking them off on his fingers.

"Naturally. The Three Musketeers," she murmured, looking at her sauce.

"Pierce and Leanna." Silas' boyfriend and Tal's girlfriend.

"Sir Lancelot and Morgana La Fey."

Warren flashed her a grin. "You didn't hear that from me. And you're mixing your archetypes again."

"That's doesn't matter, and I'm hardly blind. Who else? This girl who I assume is the best friend of someone?"

"Yes, Leanna's. Her name is Madison. She was in the school play last year, remember?"

His mother gave a little sniff that might have been simply inhaling the scent of her sauce. "Naturally. Anyone else?"

"Four others—Terry and Quin and two girls named Rachel and Katie. None of them are dating, just hanging out. But Terry and Quin said something about flowers, so I thought I should find out. Silas says never mind, and Tal says buy them all some. They're not very helpful."

His mother gave him a look that indicated she felt most teen boys were less than helpful, but then she shrugged. "I can tell you that if you don't give her a flower and the other girls get them, she'll be crushed. It's a small thing, really; what could it hurt? Is she the sort of girl who will assume it means you're interested in her?"

Warren wondered how he was supposed to know the answer to that. Girls baffled him in general, and when considered in direct relation to him, they were completely inscrutable. "Don't they all do that?" he asked, not honestly expecting a reply. Mostly he was the sort of person to stay out of situations where it would become an issue.

Slowly and with great care, his mom set aside the spoon she'd been using and put both of her hands on the counter, palms down. "Honey, you know that I want to give you privacy, and you know that you've earned my trust. But parents sometimes need to know what's going on in the lives of their young adult children, because even when something is private, it's very important for the family as a whole to be aware. Do you understand?"

Warren blinked twice, then stared at her and nodded slowly. He had no idea what was going on or how the conversation had moved from flowers to... whatever this was. Rapidly, he began to search for something in his life that could be termed both "private" and "important." He knew his grades were okay, and it wasn't like he'd ever smoked or drank or done any drugs at all. He didn't even have magazines of questionable content under his mattress, nor lotion by his bed—that's what showers were for, for the love of God. He hadn't missed curfew in months, not since he'd fallen asleep at Tal's when they were doing their take-home midterm—

"Are you gay?"

Warren gasped out a laugh. Was that all? The thing that had her gripping the countertop and talking about trust?

"Yes, of course."

That had been finally sorted out the day after Silas had gotten his first blow job (not from Dillon, who'd been an idiot) and ignored Warren's rules. The level of description had brought a lot of truths home to Warren in a hurry. He had not, in fact, handled his realization as easily or as quickly as Silas had.

Warren nodded at her and suddenly saw where the worry might be coming from. "But no one knows, and I'm neither seeing anyone nor interested in anyone."

Her eyebrows shot up. "Silas?"

His laughter turned into something more genuine. "No, Mom. Not Silas. He's my best friend and that's all. Besides, teenage boys are confusing." Not as confusing as teenage girls, perhaps, but they came with their own set of issues. "Not Silas. Not Tal, not anyone."

He wasn't sure if she looked relieved or disappointed. He was sure, however, that the relatives might not hear about the group date, but would hear all about his mom's PFLAG meetings.

"But you haven't even told him?"

Warren ate more veggies. "The thing is, Silas is really out, Mom. He started the Gay-Straight Alliance, he's got a column in the school paper, he's on the anti-bullying committee. The mayor had him come and talk to the city council, for God's sake. Silas is so high profile that he doesn't get flak, doesn't get whispered about in school, other than who is he dating this month kind of talk. I'm not interested in being like that. I'm me. I'm smart and under the radar, for the most part. But if I came out, it would be hell. And since I'm not interested in anyone, there's no point. I'll come out in college, I guess."

His mother's eyes filled with tears and she blinked them away. "It shouldn't be this way for you."

"I know." He did. Sometimes he got mad about it, but mostly he saved his energy for getting into college and getting scholarships. "It'll be different when I'm out of high school. It'll be different when I find someone worth the difficulty of coming out for."

She nodded. "I love you. I hope you find him soon; I want to meet him, too."

Warren smiled. "So. Do I buy her a corsage or not?"

"Sure, sweetie. Something pretty." She was stirring again. "And if she falls for you, you'll let her down nicely, right?"

"I'll try, Mom. I promise to try."

As it turned out, letting Madison down wasn't nearly the problem Warren had worried about. Her father, on the other hand, would need some handling if Warren ever intended to darken their door again. Which he didn't.

"So, Maddy tells me you're the class valedictorian," her father boomed. He was still holding Warren's hand from the handshake. "And that you volunteer at the food bank?" He was a huge man, in direct contradiction to how short and small his daughter was. He loomed over Warren, who at five foot eleven wasn't small.

Warren, not precisely comfortable in his tuxedo, nodded and resisted the urge to yank at his tie. "Yes, sir." Clearly more was expected as a reply, so he added, "Only twice a month, though. I have a very part-time job at a used bookstore, and the times conflict."

Her father nodded, appearing to approve. "I guess you'll be off to college in September? Valedictorian, I bet you had your pick of schools. Maddy got into three, but wants to take a year off." That, he clearly didn't approve of. "Maybe you can talk to her."

"Uh, sure." Warren nodded. "Maybe it will come up over dinner." He looked around, trying not to crane his neck to see up the staircase. "Is she almost ready?" he asked as politely as he could. He had a feeling there would be photos and stuff before they could make their escape, and they were supposed to go over to Leanna's to pick up Leanna and Tal.

"She should be—her mother's gone up to get her." He led Warren into the living room, the perfect setting for photos. "Have you picked a school yet?"

Warren nodded, his hands absently toying with the edge of the plastic clamshell box that held a corsage. "I got a full scholarship to Penn State, so I'll start there. I'll go somewhere else for my graduate degrees. Right now, being only three hours away from home sounds good."

Madison's dad looked like he was going to question the choice—and Warren didn't really want to list off all the schools he'd gotten offers from—but Madison and her mother came down then, and suddenly it was time for awkwardly posed photos and compliments that neither of them had a lot of practice with. For a group date, the evening was starting off distinctly one on one.

Warren had his mother's car, so they drove to Leanna's house to gather her and Tal, then swung by Silas' place to make sure he and Pierce weren't still trapped by Silas' mother's camera. Silas, being vocal about not being perceived as the girl, then made them all go to Pierce's house for more photos.

After dinner, during which no one talked about college, the six of them met the other four, and they headed to the hotel where the prom was being held, joining the other three hundred graduates and their dates. It took a while to actually get in, since there were yet more people to take photos, and apparently girls liked to spend an hour talking about their dresses with all the other girls. Then there was great discussion about who was going to be crowned king and queen of the senior class—an honor not nearly as high as being crowned at homecoming, but certainly nothing to sneeze at.

Warren knew who was going to be king; Silas' name was on the ballot, after all, and since it was Silas, a little thing like being queer and out wasn't going to stop it from happening.

"I'll be right back," Madison told him as they neared the doors. "If you guys make it in before we're back, just grab a table, okay?"

Warren nodded, and all the females in their party headed to the bathroom. "Why do they do that?"

"People have been asking that for generations," Tal said, sounding very knowledgeable. He looked suddenly very adult in his tuxedo and new haircut, which was about three inches shorter than it had been all through high school. "Hey, how's your speech coming?"

"It's coming." It was done, but Warren had learned not to say such things. "It's brief, I promise."

"Hey, Silas!" One of their classmates walked past, grinning and waving a camera. "Got you looking like an idiot. Again!" The yearbook was full of photos, not all of them Silas, of notable people looking bizarre.

Silas laughed and discreetly flipped him off, then went back to holding hands with Pierce. Pierce, a quiet guy who liked monster movies and hiking, took it all in stride, or at least made it look like he was totally at ease. He hadn't been out for as long as Silas, though, and sometimes Warren wondered how much of Pierce's comfort was merely just allowing Silas to sweep him along with things.

The line moved a few feet and Warren nodded to a couple of teachers who smiled at him while listening to Tal and Terry talk about summer jobs, Terry's car breaking down again, and how soon they figured they could get the girls to leave the dance so they could go have some real fun. Warren stifled a sigh at that. The after-party, a safe grad event held by the student council, was to be at the Bowl-a-Drome. The party itself would probably be fine—how bad could staying up all night eating junk food be, after all?—but the transition between the prom to the party had potential for awfulness. The ten of them were slated to go to Terry's house to change clothes and have a fast pizza, but Warren was pretty sure that more than two people in their group were hoping to take advantage of the time for traditional after-prom messing around.

Warren wondered if he could just drop Madison off, plead forgetting his clothes, and go home.

The girls came back, giggling, and they finally got into the ballroom and found a table. Madison turned to him with an intent look that Warren suspected she'd practiced.

"Would you have hurt feelings if I said that I prefer not to slow dance?"

Warren shook his head. "No." He smiled a little. "We're not dating, after all."

She looked relieved. "Right. And I would dance with you if you asked, I swear. Plus, fast dancing is fun and we can do that all night. But the thing is, I kind of have a crush on someone and want to look available, if I can. But not a wallflower. I have no idea how to do one and not the other."

"Oh, that's easy," Warren told her with another smile. "You just don't slow dance with anyone, but you don't sit and look depressed, either. When the slow music comes on, we sit and chat and look like we're solving world problems. With an empty chair between us, of course, so there's no misunderstanding."

She laughed. "Awesome. You really don't mind?"

He waved it off with one hand. "Not at all. Happy to help. Who's the crush we're going to try to ensnare?"

She looked around, peering into the dim light. "I don't see him... oh, there he is." She made a subtle gesture with her hand, hidden by her chair back. "Four o'clock, the bunch of guys by Heather Otton." Everyone knew Heather Otton, and the fact that she was in a scarlet dress helped. "Mike Koyko. Do you know him?"

Warren shook his head. "I don't think so." He studied the boys in the group. "Oh, wait. The one with the blond tips? He's in my calculus class."

She nodded. "He's really smart." She laughed again. "Not as smart as you, though, I guess."

Warren shrugged. "He seems nice enough. How about I go get us something to drink and you can set to enticing him?"

She nodded and he got up, noticing for the first time that their group had scattered. Tal and Leanna were still there, but the others had dispersed. Warren got into the line for drinks, spotted Silas and Pierce ahead of him, and nodded when Pierce caught his eye. He and Pierce hadn't spent a great deal of time together, but over the five months he'd been with Silas, Pierce had made an effort to get to know both Warren and Tal. Warren appreciated that, since mostly Silas' boyfriends had felt threatened by them. Still, it wasn't easy to really know someone when mostly you only saw them for movies or study groups.

The dance itself was fairly boring, Warren thought, but he hadn't been expecting much else. He danced a little, talked some, sat in the too-loud room for the most part. Mike Koyko wandered past at some point and stopped to chat with Madison. Warren excused himself and went to the restroom; when he came back, she was gone. He assumed that was a good thing and that he'd find out what happened later that night.

Tal and Silas and Pierce grabbed him at one point just after eleven and dragged him out to the car so he could open the trunk for them; Silas had left his camera in his duffle bag, and insisted that he needed it right then, but Warren couldn't figure out why. Pierce rolled his eyes a lot and smiled at Silas, teasing him with looks rather than words.

Warren and Tal left them by the car, kissing each other in a way that would get any of the grads stopped at the prom, gay or straight. "Don't be late for the crowning,"

Tal called back as he and Warren got a row or two away. Silas waved a hand at them.

They made it back, but only just, and Pierce looked distinctly flushed. Silas, of course, looked fine, if a little smug. When Heather Otton was crowned queen to Silas' king, no one was surprised. Pierce didn't seem bothered when the king and queen shared a dance, though he did smile when Silas came right back to him, his shiny crown slightly askew.

"Are we ready to blow this joint?" Silas asked, looking around at their group. "Warren, you lost your date."

"I know." Warren shrugged. "She's happier for it."

Leanna stood up. "I'll go tell her we'll meet her at the party—I'll take her clothes with us." She darted off into the darkness, Tal watching her go with a smile that spoke of high hopes.

Warren dug his keys out yet again. "So, we're going to Terry's?"

Terry nodded and stood up with his date, Rachel, and Quin and Katie, who'd been on the opposite side of the table from Warren when they weren't all dancing. "We'll meet you there. Ready, guys?" He led the four of them out, one arm looped around Rachel's shoulders. So much for not dating.

Warren and Silas and Pierce walked to Warren's car, knowing Tal and Leanna would catch up. "Good night?" Warren asked Silas. "I'm not ever calling you Your Majesty."

"So you think." Silas grinned at him. "Me and Pierce are taking the back seat."

"Tal's going to be back there with you."

"As long as he keeps his hands to himself, that's fine."

Warren rolled his eyes and unlocked the car. He got in and started it up so he could play with the stereo while ignoring the sounds of Silas and Pierce making out. Some things a best friend just had to endure.

Thankfully they hadn't gotten beyond a few kisses and some laughing before Tal and Leanna arrived. Leanna insisted on sitting between them, which made Warren and Tal laugh with delight, and the five of them went off to Terry's to change their clothes and eat pizza. Leanna's mission to arrange things with Madison had given Terry's group enough time to get home, so the lights were on and the house was welcoming when they arrived.

Terry's mom let them in and told them where they could all change—the girls taking turns in her bedroom and bathroom, the boys scattered all over the house in bedrooms and the basement family room—and said the pizzas were on their way. Terry appeared in jeans and T-shirt, so Warren took his room and changed quickly, wanting to get out of the way as fast as he could. He hoped that someone with authority was keeping an eye on things; Tal and Leanna were on the same floor, after all, though Silas and Pierce had been separated by circumstance and Tal being pushy.

When Warren was in his jeans and a loose shirt, he packed his tux into the garment bag and took his things out to the car. The trunk was empty, so it should hold all four tuxedos lying flat, and he planned to return them all on his way home in the morning. He was about to close the trunk and go inside when Pierce came out with his suit slung over his arm.

"Hey," Warren greeted him, waiting while Pierce put his garment bag on top of Warren's. "All set for phase two?"

"Sure." Pierce smiled at him, his gaze darting away and then back, like he was a little shy. "Are you?" He was looking at Warren through lowered eyelashes.

"I guess." Warren put his hands into his pockets and took a small step backward. "Should be a good time.

Here, I mean. Pizza, fewer people to share it with."

Pierce laughed. "So true," he said. He put one hand on Warren's arm. "Can I ask you something, Warren?" The look was now steady, and Warren was distinctly uncomfortable.

"Um, yeah. Okay." He looked toward the house. Where was Silas? He really should come and collect his boyfriend.

"It's okay if you don't want to tell me. Silas says he's known you forever and that you've never once said anything about liking someone—a girl or a guy. Is that true?" The hand, mercifully, moved away and off his arm.

Warren shrugged. It wasn't Pierce's business at all, but it seemed rude to say so—even more rude than Pierce asking. "I've been real busy with school and work and stuff, I guess. You know me, nose always in a book."

"I know." Pierce nodded and moved a little closer. They were still behind the car, and when Warren backed away from Pierce, he lost his view of the front door. "But here's the thing. I think you do like someone. I think that when you watch me kissing Silas, when you think about it, you get turned on." Pierce didn't seem upset by it.

Warren lifted an eyebrow. "What on earth makes you think that?" Warren had made it a mission to utterly ignore it, after all. His non-reaction was perfect.

"Oh, just a couple things. You don't sigh and roll your eyes and get obnoxious the way Tal does, for one."

"Tal's more of a drama queen than Silas is," Warren pointed out. This time he didn't move away when Pierce stepped forward. He was at least two inches taller than Pierce, and he liked the height advantage.

"That's true," Pierce admitted. His voice had grown soft. "But Tal's very, very het. And you are very, very not." The hand was back. "I think that if Silas wasn't your best friend, you'd be all over me like an eager puppy on a bone."

Warren stared at him hard for moment, his brain trying to catch up with Pierce's words. Then he started to laugh, the sound startling and loud in the late-night air. He laughed and he laughed, one hand curling around his belly to hold his sides. The idea of it was so surreal and out of tune with his life that he couldn't react in any other way. He saw Pierce's look grow puzzled and then angry, only the barest flash of mortification flicking between the two. And yet, he couldn't stop laughing.

"What's the joke?" Silas asked cheerfully, coming around the car and tossing his tuxedo bag on top of the others. "Was it about Heather's dress? Because, Lord willing, I will never be so close to so much cleavage again."

"Nothing," Pierce said shortly, backing up a step.

Warren found his voice. "Your boyfriend is a funny guy," he said, patting Silas on the arm. "He'll tell you all about it later, I'm sure." That should be suitable punishment for the little louse. Warren walked away, still chuckling. As if he'd ever want to get with someone dating his best friend. As if he'd ever want to get with *Pierce,* of all people. There hadn't been anything wrong with Pierce, sure, but he was hardly someone Warren would go for.

No, Warren knew what he was looking for. Someone bright. Someone with a work ethic, someone with goals. A sense of humor was important, and a love of books. Warren was looking for a person who wouldn't hit on his boyfriend's buddies.

He hoped Silas wouldn't keep Pierce long, although maybe Pierce would leave, after humiliating himself.

Suddenly, eating pizza sounded like a party in and of itself. Warren went inside, looking for Terry and the others.

Tal sat in his graduation robes and looked around. The speeches were boring, for the most part, and the day was hot. At least they got to have the ceremony inside in the air conditioning. The arena was barely big enough for them all and their parents, but they managed to fit in. He could see the back of Silas' head a row ahead of him and down a few people, too far away to talk to. Warren was on the stage, sitting next to other people making speeches.

It had been a week since the prom. A week filled with events and parties and running around getting final grades and his dad proudly telling everyone that Tal had made the honor roll. Somewhere in there, he'd managed to find an evening to hang out in Silas' garage with just him and Warren, and that had been the best night of the week. The three of them just fit right, and they laughed and messed around and packed a few things away for Silas' mom.

Tal wondered if they'd be able to take that sense of right with them as they all moved north. They were going to Penn State, which was cool, but in different departments. The idea of the three of them getting an apartment had blown up in the face of money and what scholarships would cover for Warren; the dorms worked out to be cheaper anyway.

Someone new got up to speak, and Tal looked around for Leanna. She wasn't going to Penn State, but was heading off to some little liberal arts college in Massachusetts. She seemed pretty excited. She also seemed unthrilled with the idea of a long-term, long-distance relationship. The end was in sight, if he was honest with himself, but he really liked her and he thought she liked him well enough, too. They'd have the summer and it would end sweetly, he hoped.

With sex, maybe. That would be good.

He also thought he might see an end in sight for Silas and Pierce, but wasn't sure why. Warren didn't know, either, and didn't have anything to say on the matter. Tal had thought that Warren and Pierce got on all right, overall, but they hadn't said more than hello all week. Warren got along with everyone, ever since he'd stopped saying out loud who wasn't working to their academic potential. He'd been broken of that years ago, and since he was usually willing to tutor anyone who asked, no one minded that he was a brainiac. Still, something weird was going on with Silas and Pierce, and Tal wanted to know what.

Tal also wanted to know when, exactly, Warren was going to acknowledge the elephant in the room. It was completely clear that Warren wasn't into girls and never would be, but after two years of being a part of the GSA and supporting Silas, it would be nice if Warren would take the last step and hoist his flag.

Maybe Tal would give him one as a grad present.

Maybe Tal would take his mother's advice and mind his own business. That would be a change, though, and why start then?

The speaker sat down and Tal applauded politely. The crowd was growing a little restless. "When are we going up for our diplomas?" he whispered to the girl sitting next to him.

"Right after the next speech." She pointed to where they were on the program. "Valedictorian Address."

Tal sat up straight, fully at attention.

"You seem excited," she said dryly.

"Shh. Best friend."

"Oh. I guess someone has to be." She craned her neck. "He's kind of cute."

"Cuter than me?" He didn't even glance at her; the question was pure reflex.

"No, I guess not."

He grinned.

Warren, at the podium, cleared his throat and went through addressing all the people who needed addressing, from the principal to the parents and all the special guests in between. Then he settled into the speech, speaking clearly and concisely about the joy of graduation, the achievement they should all be proud of, and the goals they looked forward to in the coming months and years. He did a good job, Tal thought. He wasn't overly sentimental, and he wasn't brutal about how this was, after all, just high school and really just a baseline for people like him, who were heading off to multiple degrees, no doubt. He mentioned the cafeteria staff by name, which was nice, and then he finished up in less than three minutes with a challenge to live lives that they could barely dream about, to seek out their hearts' fondest wishes, and to come back in ten years to share their further success.

All in all, it was a nice speech, and Warren got a huge round of applause—probably for keeping it short.

An hour and a half later, diploma and math award in hand, Tal pushed through the crowd to find Warren and Silas, standing with their mothers.

"Ladies," Tal said, bowing to them both. "You look lovely, as always."

Silas' mom rolled her eyes, but Warren's mother smiled at him. "I'm going to miss you, Tal." She kissed Warren on the cheek. "Don't take too long, dear. Your grandparents want to spend as much time with you as they can." She moved off and Silas' mother went with her, the two of them chatting about survival and some kind of fight that had yogurt and cheese.

"I lost track of your awards," Silas said to Warren. "Five?"

"Four. Tal got journalism. And you did well—how much money?"

Silas shrugged but looked pleased. He'd won a

community involvement prize and a volunteer award. "About eight hundred, give or take."

"Nice." Tal was impressed. His journalism prize from the Kiwanis Club was worth two hundred and fifty. "I'm hoping I can buy a textbook with mine."

Warren smiled. "You will. So, see you guys tomorrow? I have family now."

Tal and Silas nodded. "All day. Hiking? No bodies."

"If someone is bringing food, I'm there." Warren grinned. "We did it."

"We sure as hell did." Silas grabbed Warren and hugged him, then pulled Tal in. "We did."

Tal smiled. This was the best part. The three of them were always the best part.

Chapter Five

Some Strange Awakening

The first semester at college was not unlike the last semester of high school, Warren thought. He was working far harder than everyone else, and everyone else was hunting down the next party. The dorm was noisy for the first week, then the quiet hours took effect, to his great relief.

He got along with his roommate, who seemed to appreciate having someone who spent most of his time in the library. For the most part their room was tolerably neat; it was too small to get messy without causing tripping. His roommate also had a girlfriend, one dorm over, so was often gone until ten or eleven at night.

Warren and Tal were on the same floor, but Silas was a level down; it wasn't terribly inconvenient, especially with cellphones and free Wi-Fi in the building. They managed to spend most of the first weeks together before their programs started taking up all their time.

Silas, to no one's surprise, was getting his degree in business with an eye to start-ups and entrepreneurship. Tal was taking a cross section of liberal arts classes, trying to get a broad foundation to move into communications in his second year, and Warren was focusing on sociological theory, but had to fill in a lot of electives the first year. He picked two statistics classes for fun.

Generally speaking, college was exactly what all three of them were ready for, in almost every sense. Silas and Tal were ready to spread their wings and live away from home; Warren was ready for an environment in which the words "I need to study all weekend" were understood.

The first time Warren had sex, it was the exact, complete, and direct opposite of anything he had ever imagined happening to him. There weren't even any books involved.

On the Friday afternoon the week before final exams and the winter break, Warren returned to his room from the library late in the day. His head was full of his sociology class and the very nebulous idea of doing some research on social networking sites across economic boundaries, and he barely nodded to his roommate when he came in. He'd unpacked half his bag before he realized his roommate wasn't there and the boy on the bed was a stranger.

"Uh, hello." Warren gave him a long look. "Who are you?"

"Nick." Nick was sitting on the edge of the bed, his ball cap keeping his eyes hidden. He could have looked up, but didn't. "I'm Stephen's brother. He's gone to get us some food. You're Warren?" He looked up then, showing off a dark bruise around his eye. "Sorry to land on you this way."

Warren winced and went back to unpacking. "Nice shiner. Are you staying the weekend?" Stephen had said he had a brother, but somehow Warren had pictured something different than this. They seemed to be very close to the same age, and Nick might even be a few years older. He was cute, aside from the black eye.

"No, just tonight. I gotta go home and deal with this, you know?" He gestured to his eye. "I got jumped, and my mom wanted me out of the area for a couple days. I came here instead of going to our grandparents. Our little brother is freaked out."

Warren frowned and sat down. "That sounds tense." Okay, different brother. "Why'd you get jumped?"

Nick shrugged, looking down again. "Hit on the wrong person, I guess." His phone chirped at him and he took the call. "Stephen, hey. Warren's home. Are you on your way?" He paused to listen, and Warren got himself organized for his evening of studying. It was too close to finals to take a night off, and he wanted to write down his idea before it slipped away.

"Hey, sorry again." Nick was standing. "I'm going down to meet Stephen and his girl. Have a good night, and it was nice to meet you."

Warren stood up and offered his hand. "You, too. Sorry about your trouble. I expect I'll see you later on."

Nick shook his hand and left, moving like he had more pains than his black eye.

Three hours later, Warren was surrounded by notes, his earphones were in, and his MP3 player was filling his world with the sound of wind in leaves. He couldn't study to music, and he couldn't study to the clamor of the dorm, but he found he could study to the noise-reducing headphones and the sounds of nature. The only downside was that he had to keep his phone on vibrate and on his body or he'd never get a single call or text message, which would lead to Silas and Tal hunting him down and being very cranky at him.

The door opened and he looked up, waving as Stephen and Nick came in. He took out his headphones with one hand, still writing with the other one. "Hey. I can pack up if you guys need to talk or something."

Stephen shook his head and shifted his weight from one foot to the other. "No, stay. Nick wants to talk to you, if that's okay. It's all right if it's not—I can sneak him into the other dorm or something for the night." He glared at his brother. "One night."

"Me?" Warren looked at Nick. "Why?"

Nick looked at his brother. "Go on. I'll call you later if I need to, or if Warren gives me the boot." Nick was strangely calm and a lot more confident than he had seemed earlier. "It'll be okay. I'll be out of your hair by tomorrow afternoon."

"Exams," Stephen said pointedly, which almost made Warren laugh. He had yet to see Stephen study, although it was possible he had been studying in his girlfriend's room. "Text me later, even if Warren doesn't kick you out." To Warren, he added, "Which you should feel perfectly free to do. It's okay. Really."

Warren was far too curious to do any booting without getting more information first. "I'll keep it in mind," he promised. "You're going to Natalie's?"

Stephen nodded and went to the door. "Be good, Nick." Then he left.

Still surrounded by his papers, Warren looked at Nick and nodded toward the other bed. "Have a seat. I admit you've got me interested."

"Yeah. Me, too." Nick sat down across from him. "I got this eye from hitting on a guy." He pointed at his eye and shook his head. "No, that's not true. I got this eye from not saying no when a guy hit on me, and for leaving a club with him."

Warren felt his stomach drop. "It was a set-up." He'd heard the horror stories. Silas had told Warren the worst ones he'd heard, and from his volunteering, he'd heard a lot. "How many of them hurt you?"

"Two or three." Nick shrugged. He unzipped his

hoodie and took it off, then lifted the hem of his T-shirt. "This bruise and my eye were the only damage. I'd say they weren't trying very hard, but mostly they were just stupid and started beating on me too soon. They were right in the parking lot, in plain view. The bouncer ran them off, and the off-duty cop they keep around to watch the lot got one of them almost before the second punch landed. Of course, the story is that I was mocking them inside the building and calling someone's girl a whore."

"Of course." Warren sighed. "You got off easy, I'm afraid. Why's your little brother freaked?"

"He figures they're going to come back at me again. I can't seem to get him to believe that they weren't targeting me; I just happened to be the guy they caught."

"Stephen believes you, though?" Warren gathered up the papers he knew he was done with and stacked them neatly on his pillow.

"Yeah, he gets it." Nick nodded.

"Well, that's good." Warren leaned back against the wall. "How come you wanted to talk to me about it?"

Nick smiled at him. "I wanted to get your reaction. Which was good. Very good."

"Why?"

Nick's smile grew. "Are you seeing anyone?"

"No." This was absurd. He should be rolling his eyes and pointing Nick to the door. But he wasn't. He really wasn't. He was gathering up the rest of his papers and telling his stomach to settle the hell down.

"Stephen tells me that you're wicked smart."

"Stephen's right." Warren shrugged. "But it's all about books. That's all."

"Oh, I don't know." Nick hadn't moved. Not even an inch, but there was a lot less air in the room and Warren had somehow cleaned off his bed. "Pop quiz."

"They're my specialty." Warren took his stack of

papers and books and put them on his desk, not even having to get off the bed to do it. Then his phone came out of his pocket and went on the charger, and the earphones got tossed on the chair. "Ready."

"What does a smart guy plus a slightly damaged guy plus twelve hours in town equal?"

Warren smiled. "Easy. A locked door and a text to the two people who could ruin it, saying I'm going to sleep and getting up at four to study, if they want to meet me. They won't."

Nick blinked. "No one would."

"Exactly." Warren got up and went to the door, making sure it was locked. Then he sent a text to Silas and Tal, who both immediately sent back laughing reactions. "That's taken care of." To his great surprise, he was still standing up, and he wasn't even shaking like a leaf. "You should know, however, that I usually study instead of putting out for strangers."

"That's perfectly fine." Nick stood up too and moved right in front of him. He was an inch shorter than Warren and probably three inches broader. His arms were defined and strong. Warren thought that whoever'd jumped him had been a complete idiot. After the shock of surprise, Nick could probably have taken them all apart. He put one hand on Warren's hip, his thumb right on Warren's hipbone. "I'll walk you through it."

Warren nodded. "I expect you will." He looked at Nick's eyes. Even the one that was swollen and bruised looked pretty. "You know, I would have tried to pick you up in that club. But without the posse in the parking lot."

Nick smiled at him, showing even, white teeth. "Really?"

"For sure." It was easy to fall into a fantasy life if they only had twelve hours.

"Cool. Don't tell my brother about this, okay? Tell

him we had a long heart-to-heart about how horrible jocks are or something."

Warren laughed. "Trust me. Totally not telling your brother. Or anyone, I expect. This is for me." He thought about that for a moment and suddenly relaxed. "This is for me."

"And me." The thumb on Warren's hip moved and Nick's smile grew. "There you are. Welcome to the party."

Warren nodded once, dipped his head, and kissed Nick's mouth, not being shy about it. He knew what not to do, and it was surprisingly easy to kiss someone who you knew wasn't going to reject you.

And, as it turned out, fun.

Warren wasn't sure how it happened, but within a few moments they were lying down on his bed, still kissing. They weren't doing anything *but* kissing, but he was okay with that, and Nick seemed to be, too. There were tiny little kisses, and there were kisses that felt like Nick was taking an extended tour of Warren's mouth, and they were all really, really great. Warren had no idea what to do with his hands, and one was kind of squished under Nick's shoulder, but when he put the other one in Nick's hair and tilted Nick's head with it, he got a moan, so he counted that as good, too.

After a while, and a lot more kisses, Nick whispered, "Okay?" and Warren nodded. It was okay; he was okay; it was okay to go on. Whatever, it was all most certainly okay. Nick smiled and kissed him again, easing Warren to his back.

Warren, to his great surprise, went. No hesitation, nothing. Just a nod and yeah, it's okay and there he was, on his back with a cute guy licking at his neck and kissing him and pushing a warm hand up his shirt to pet his belly. "Yes." He blinked at the ceiling and then laughed. "Yeah, okay. Yes." He pushed at Nick until he could struggle up, dragging his shirt off.

Nick looked delighted and tugged his T-shirt off as well. "Bonus points to you. Pop quizzes really are your thing, huh?"

"I'm surprisingly good under pressure." Warren touched Nick's bruise. "I'm sorry they hurt you."

"I'm glad I came here to get away from it."

Warren smiled and Nick kissed him again, this time both of them using their hands to trace lines or muscles or air currents. Warren's head was tipped back to let Nick use his tongue along Warren's collarbone when their hips shifted and things heated up. He'd been aware of his own erection, of course, but in an oddly abstract way. That changed when Nick's was there, too, the two of them lined up by intent or by accident.

Warren gasped and his hands dug into Nick's back.

"There we go," Nick said, lifting his head. "Nice." He rocked, very gently, and made Warren gasp again. Before Warren could say anything or even really get his breath back, Nick was kissing him again and moving up and off. Warren held on, not able to protest around Nick's tongue, and then protest died away under Nick's hand.

"Thank God for button fly." Nick tore at Warren's jeans and then there was a warm hand around Warren's cock, and it wasn't his hand at all, not even close.

Warren couldn't speak. Part of his brain was completely disgusted with his lack of cool, but most of it was having a great time. He closed his eyes and breathed, tried to sort out what he wanted to do. Distantly, he was aware that Nick was waiting for him. In a moment and two breaths later, he opened his eyes. "Okay. Back now."

Nick laughed softly and stroked his cock, once. "Twelve hours covers a lot of recovery time. You're okay."

Warren nodded. "Kiss me."

"Is that really what you want?" Nick looked at what he his hand was doing. "Really, really?"

Warren nodded again. "No."

"I have a better idea."

Warren was sure he did. When Nick dipped his head, Warren closed his eyes again and prayed he'd hang on long enough to enjoy this.

As Nick's tongue stroked along the underside of his cock, Warren's hips lifted. Nick took it and tugged down Warren's jeans as well, proving his talents as completely as Warren could have asked for.

Once more, Warren didn't know what to do with his hands. He put one on Nick's shoulder and the other on his own hip, mostly because his brain was starting to short out. Nick's mouth was warm and wet and there was a tingling sensation all up and down his spine that was far too familiar. "Oh, no. No, no, no." He didn't know he'd said it out loud until Nick was off him, squeezing hard at Warren's cock with one fist and pulling his balls back down with the other hand.

"Shh, it's okay. Plenty of time." Nick waited for Warren to calm a bit and then kissed his mouth, the movement awkward given their positions. "Ready?"

Warren nodded. "Sorry."

"Don't be sorry. You're awesome." Nick grinned at him. "I figure you're gonna go pretty fast, then I'm going to take an hour building you back up again. You're not going to make your four a.m. studying, Warren."

Warren swallowed. "I have a week until my exams."

Nick laughed and went down on him again, his mouth hot and somehow even more perfect. Nick licked and sucked and used his hand to stroke until Warren was almost bucking on the bed, unable to keep his hips still. He had one hand tangled in the blanket under him, and the other he was holding in a fist, almost wanting to bite it to keep quiet. He looked down, watching his cock slide into Nick's mouth, and groaned.

Nick looked up at him and winked. Then he took Warren's fisted hand and put it on his own head, the signal clear enough that even Warren got the point. He groaned again, laid his hand flat on Nick's head, and fucked his mouth. It would have been astounding if it hadn't been his first blow job and he hadn't been seconds away from coming; as it was, it was merely awesome. He pushed in until he couldn't hold off any longer, then let go, giving Nick barely a second to get out of the way.

Warren came all over his stomach, his cock in Nick's hand and Nick's tongue on his balls. "Oh, God. Yes." He lay back, panting. His leg was shaking for some reason.

Nick laughed softly and rolled away. "Easy," he said when Warren jerked toward him. "Not going anywhere." He got undressed and yanked Warren's jeans and socks off the rest of the way. Somehow Warren had lost track of his boxer briefs. He assumed they were there, somewhere. Nick got back on the bed and looked around, then passed Warren the box of tissues to use to clean up. "Nicely done."

Warren didn't trust himself to speak. When he'd mopped up a suitable amount he reached for Nick and kissed him, feeling lazy and perfect and warm. Then he got brave and curled his fingers around Nick's prick.

"Oh, nice." Nick wiggled down beside him. "Go for it. You've got great hands."

Warren laughed. "I have normal hands." He explored, though, lifting and weighing and tracing until Nick's cock lifted up off his belly. Then Warren took him in hand and stroked the way he liked it—not shy, not tentative, not rushed. Just a good grip, attention to detail, and a little bit of lube via a licked palm.

Nick grunted and thrust into his hand. "Oh, yeah.

You know what to do."

"Tell me if you want something else." The angle was totally bizarre, but he could manage it. Clearly.

"No, this is good." Nick was breathing harder, faster, and one of his legs crooked up so his foot could give him some leverage. "Uh-huh."

Warren looked at what he was doing and swept a bead of fluid around the head with his thumb. "You've got a great cock," he said, meaning it. It wasn't huge, but it was nice and thick, and it fit his hand just fine. "Can I suck you later?"

Nick came in short jerks, come streaking across Warren's fingers and wrist. "Yeah. Yeah, you can."

"Nice." Warren reached for more tissue, reasonably sure that his studying was shot until Sunday, at least.

Chapter Six

Intervention

Silas waited years before his patience snapped and he took his first definitive steps to find out what was going on. He would never have thought it possible, and if he hadn't had Tal to talk it all over with for those years, he might not have lasted. Curiosity had always had a hold of him, but Tal had convinced him not to be nosy and that Warren was the type of person who needed his privacy.

Two and a half years at college was enough, and Silas picked his time carefully. Well, impulsively, but he felt good about it.

The night Warren turned twenty-one was going to be a night of answers. No doubt he'd hoped that the event would slide on by under everyone's radar, but of course Silas wasn't going to let that happen.

Silas was all about celebrations, after all.

After their first year of college, Silas had them celebrating that they'd survived the year with none of them failing anything, that they were still friends who hung out at least weekly if not more, and that their burgeoning social lives were merely burgeoning and not yet life-changing or life-challenging.

Well, any more life-changing than coming out had been, anyway. As a standard to beat, it was pretty high. In short, it was a Dear God We Lived party.

From there, in their second year, Silas had celebrated Tal's four months in a row of being single (his first long stretch since grade ten), then his starting to date a chemistry student named Olivia Demers who was deemed both interesting and cool by Warren and Silas. Olivia had deemed them interesting and tolerable, too, so the four of them hung out a lot. She was pretty and refined, tall, and strong enough to take on Tal's ridiculous dedication to fitness. She was also black, and very occasionally that attracted looks and whispers, but she handled it well; better than Tal, who had a tendency to get pissed off.

Also celebrated that second year was Silas' revival of the gay support group on campus, and Warren's surprising entrance into college social life by joining the theater group backstage and working on acquiring better props. Tal joined the newspaper, since it took less time than acting, and before long they'd become fully immersed in campus life. There were grades to celebrate, survival they couldn't take for granted, and a multitude of other high points, and they flew into their third year at college feeling like they'd gotten a grip on what it was all about and how to get there. There were classes and meetings, and in Warren's case extra classes and his independent project about social media and economic status; Warren was at college to work, and work he did.

But turning twenty-one was a big deal, and Silas was going to leverage the hell out of it. He refused to believe that Warren had reached the age of twenty-one without a personal relationship, and Silas was going to find out what the hell was going on, and with who.

It called for a plan, and it called for subtlety. Lacking

someone with both, he roped Tal in, which wasn't hard since Tal was as interested at Silas.

"First of all," Tal said, making himself at home in Silas' dorm room, "we need to clear our motives. Or at least rationalize them enough that no pesky conscience voices pop up."

"You'd be amazed how often that doesn't happen to me," Silas told him. He sat at his roommate's desk and very carefully touched nothing at all. His roommate was a little bit of a priss.

"Not really." Tal grinned. "So, we're going to drag the truth out of him, right? Pry into his most personal of personal details?"

"Yup." Silas nodded. They totally were. "Because we're his friends. Because we should know. Because it will do him good to finally let his secret out." Silas hated secrets.

"Are you hurt that he hasn't told you himself?"

"Yes." Silas didn't hesitate. "Of course I am. I mean, I came out to him the day I worked it out for myself. To both of you. And he's lying to us by omission. Also, it bothers me that if he's having dates and stuff, if he's out there making it with anyone, he's not sharing that with us. Not sharing happy stuff is too close to shame." Silas frowned. "But it doesn't feel like shame. Not Warren."

Tal shook his head. "I don't think so, either. Honestly, I think it's just become a habit. And he needs to break it."

Silas thought about that for a moment. "So we're agreed—we're going to harass him for his own good and not feel guilt."

"Right." Tal grinned. "Do you have a plan?"

"Booze."

Tal laughed. "It won't take much."

"Also part of the plan." Warren was famous for being a lightweight. Tal had managed to hide how much of a lightweight he was, and Silas, for some reason, managed to go without drinking at all most of the time without anyone even noticing. Probably because he was so full of energy all the time anyway, but in any event he wasn't going to complain if he managed to avoid hangovers. "And, most importantly, just us." That part might be trickier.

"No Olivia?"

"No Olivia." Silas winced. "Well, maybe Olivia can come for dinner. But really, when we start grilling him, she probably shouldn't be there, you know? He's not going to say anything at all if it's not just us."

Tal was nodding. "No, you're right. She'll get it." Tal shrugged. "I haven't given her details or anything, but I've told her we know he's gay but he's not talking about it. She knows it's a thing."

"Okay." Olivia was cool. "Tell her we're taking him out for his birthday, then. She's got her crowd to hang with." It wasn't a huge crowd, but Olivia had come to college with her best girlfriends, something else that worked in her favor. She never minded when Tal was all about hanging out and watching movies with Silas and Warren.

"So, Friday night?"

"Friday night. Showdown. I'll buy the beer." Silas' roommate might be a priss, but he was also twenty-one and would pick it up without any comment as long as Silas was good about keeping the room clean.

"Cool. Now, as long as we're talking about Warren, who do you think he's been getting with? That guy who does the lights for the theater group?"

"Are you kidding me?" Silas rolled his eyes. "He's nowhere near classy enough for Warren."

"But he's also not an actor, nor is he... uh, showy." Tal spoke delicately. Silas' last boyfriend, gone only two weeks, had been so flamboyant he could have had his own light show.

Silas tried not to blush. "He was over the top, but he was really, really hot," he protested. "The things he could do with his tongue would make you—"

"No, thank you!" Tal held up a hand. "No visuals."

"Talking is not visual," Silas protested.

"Ever hear of a thing called radio?" Tal shook his head. "Do not tell me what he did to you with his tongue, okay?"

"Okay." Silas grinned. "Can I tell you what he did with his hands?"

"No."

"His cock?"

"Do you want me to tell you what I do with my cock?"

Silas thought about that for a moment. "No. I really don't. Mostly out of respect for Olivia, though."

Tal laughed. "I'll pass that along. So, no idea who Warren's messing with? Ever? I'm pretty sure no one in high school."

Silas knew that was true, by inference more than fact finding. "No, not in high school. I thought maybe his first roommate, but then he left 'cause his girl got knocked up."

"Doesn't mean he wasn't giving Warren a hand," Tal said, rummaging through the clutter on Silas' desk.

Silas blinked. He wasn't sure what brought him up short, the idea that Warren would sleep with someone who had a girlfriend or the sudden image of Warren being with someone, a hand down Warren's jeans. Up until that very moment, the entire issue had been totally cerebral and theoretical. Suddenly it was a loaded gun.

"Not that I think he was," Tal was going on, making a paperclip chain with the ones he'd found. Silas thought maybe he'd taken a couple from completed assignments, too. "That guy was a jock, and Warren's more the book type."

"Warren is the book type," Silas said absently. Most of his brain was being taken up by the idea of Warren having other-person-induced orgasms. "He might like another type, something exciting to him instead of just like him."

"The guy was an engineering student."

"Good point." Warren didn't run with the engineers. He was more into hard sciences and theater and social sciences and literature students. Everyone except engineers and business students, really. Silas sighed. "I'm pretty sure he's not a virgin anymore, and I'm more than sure he's gay. I just want him to open up, for his sake."

Tal nodded slowly and dropped the chain on top of the desk clutter. "I agree. He's not sharing and that can't be healthy." He gave Silas a look that was more than a little uncomfortable. "This isn't just because we're nosy, right?"

"No." Silas was firm. "We might be nosy, but I've known him since he was five. Warren is a talker. He might still just be sharing stuff with his mom, but that makes it even worse. We're gonna round that boy up and make him remember that we're his friends and we not only want to know, but we've earned the right to be in the loop."

Tal nodded again and sighed. "He might get mad."

"He might. I'm okay with that, as long as he listens to us. If he hears us out and still chooses to keep things from us, then we can't do anything about it and will have to accept it as the way Warren is. Same as we accept that he'll probably never have any interest in owning a TV for anything other than watching movies on."

Tal snorted. "He uses his computer for that now. I doubt if he'll ever have a TV."

"Then he can't ever share a place with me." Silas grinned. "I'm gonna have a huge TV. Massive."

"I'm shocked. Really." Tal stood up. "Okay, Friday night. I'll tell Olivia, you tell Warren, and we'll go somewhere nice to soften him up. A Warren-style place."

"Not fast food is what you're saying."

"Right." Tal nodded, gave him a half-wave, and opened the door. "See you later. I have to get to class."

Silas waved back and moved to his own side of the room to make a list. He had planning to do.

Dinner itself went well; there was very little that could go wrong with good Indian food, especially when the place was tiny and full of Indians. Silas made it a rule to eat ethnic food where the people themselves preferred to find it. Warren seemed pleased with the meal and the presents—books, of course—and was in good spirits when the three of them went back to Silas' dorm room.

"Where's he?" Tal asked, pointing to the other bed.

"Gone home for the weekend." Silas opened the tiny dorm fridge and passed out beer bottles. "But he did a beer run first."

Tal grinned and lifted his bottle to Warren. "Happy birthday."

"Thanks." Warren saluted back and dropped down onto Silas' bed. He always avoided the other side of the room, not wanting to be party to any roommate issues. "So, what are we doing? It's early. Movies? Going out?"

"Staying in," Silas and Tal said at the same time. Silas opened the cupboard above his desk and showed off bags of chips. "We have provisions." He took his roommate's bed and made himself comfortable, sitting with his back to the wall. "How's rehearsal going?"

"Not bad." Warren told them about the current show he was working on, skipping the details about the play but passing along a lot of backstage gossip. Tal and Silas sucked it all up, along with more beer, and then shared gossip of their own, mostly about guys in their dorm.

Silas was speaking, but he wasn't really able to keep up with the conversation. He couldn't remember the last time he'd felt so keyed up and tense, though it might have been back when he was just starting to date. He'd been in a more scattered state than this when he came out, but not by much.

The potential for this conversation to blow up on him was suddenly looking huge. The last thing he wanted was for Warren to be upset or even angry with him. Maybe he and Tal were totally out of line after all. What if Warren got up and left and didn't come back? What if this was a boundary within their friendship that he really shouldn't cross?

Maybe Warren really was a virgin at twenty-one and would be totally humiliated by him and Tal digging into it.

Silas drank deeply, mouthful after mouthful.

"Whoa. Dude. Slow down." Warren peered at him from across the room. "What's up?"

"Nothing." Silas knew he spoke too quickly, so he followed it up with a shrug and a grin. "Nothing," he repeated.

"Mmm." Warren raised an eyebrow at him. "You lie for crap." He looked at Tal, sprawled in Silas' chair and poking away at Silas' laptop. "Hey. What's up with Silas?"

Silas tried to get Tal to shut up, but Tal didn't look up to see Silas' face at all. "He—well, we—want to talk to you about something. He's more nervous than I am 'cause it's about sex."

Warren choked on beer. He didn't spit it, though, and nothing shot out his nose, so Silas called it a win. "Sex? Seriously? I've been telling you both to shut up about sex for five years, at least. Longer in your case."

"I'm precocious," Tal said, grinning.

"You're insatiable. I don't know how Olivia puts up with you." Warren sniffed. He was very fond of Olivia, Silas thought. "Why do you want to talk to me about sex? I know what parts go where and all that, and I even know how babies are made and how to avoid that."

Silas couldn't speak. Never before had he felt like his tongue was literally tied in a knot. He looked at Tal.

"For the love of God." Tal looked back, rolled his eyes, and then sighed. "Okay, fine. You owe me a lot of beer, Silas." He turned in the chair to look directly at Warren. "Want another one?"

Warren finished his current bottle and nodded. "Yes, I think I do. I get the feeling I'll need it."

Tal reached into the fridge and tossed one to him, and then one to Silas. "So, essentially, we're wondering when you're going to think it's time to include your friends in your life a little more. We know you're a private guy—you always have been. That's cool. But now it feels like you're hiding, and we're pretty sure you don't want to do that."

Warren drank from his beer bottle but otherwise didn't move. Silas had expected him to draw up his legs or something, but he stayed where he was, mostly just lounging. Taking that as a good sign, Silas relaxed a tiny bit.

"How does that relate to sex?" Warren asked. Then he shook his head. "No, scratch that. I know what you want to know, and I guess I should thank you for not being all up in my shit before now. But do we really need to do this intervention kind of deal?"

Silas nodded. "I thought so." He cleared his throat. "I did. Because you're not showing any signs of telling us at all, and it's starting to... grate." He stopped himself from saying "hurt," knowing that Warren didn't need a pile of guilt on top of things.

Warren sighed and drank beer. "It's a lot easier to just stay quiet," he finally said. "No one ever asks, no one expects anything. I'm not very good with people, you guys. No one questions anything when I don't bring a date to parties—or even when I don't go to parties. I'm just that nerdy book guy with the good grades. It's all fine with me."

"We're not just rabble, though, are we?" Tal asked softly. "We're the guys who've had your back for years. We're the ones you can tell, and the ones you *should* tell. I know you just haven't gotten around to it and you're probably intending to do it when you finally need to, like when the right person comes along and is important enough for you to care about. But you know what? It's okay to say something before that. And it's important to, so you're, like, a whole person or some shit like that."

Warren was looking at the bottle in his hands, his face serious. Silas couldn't see his eyes, but he knew the look; Warren was thinking hard, planning what to say.

"Warren." Silas moved, intending only to sit on the edge of the roommate's bed but somehow crossing the room to sit next to Warren. "Warren. Do you trust me?"

"Of course." Warren's head snapped up. "Of course I do."

"Talk to me." Silas resisted the urge to actually hold Warren's hand.

Warren stared at him, his eyes huge. "But you know."

"Say it." From experience, Silas knew it made a difference, at least the first few times.

Warren swallowed, not looking away from him. Tal's

chair creaked. "I won't be out getting any girls pregnant," he said. "I'm gay."

Silas grinned at him, his whole body going warm. "Good job." Then he leaned forward and kissed Warren's mouth. "Well done."

Tal made a gagging sound and started to laugh. Warren blinked at him a few times, looking stunned. "You kissed me."

Silas nodded and moved back to the other bed. "I give rewards." His knees were weak and he tried not to show it. "Totally planned that, too."

"Liar," Tal said with a fake cough. "Can we move on to the next part of the intervention?"

"More drinking?" Warren asked hopefully.

"Hell, no, son. Well, yes. Drinking. But we want names and dates, boy. Names and dates."

Warren snorted and eyed Silas suspiciously. "No."

"No?"

"*Hell*, no. And don't call me 'son' or 'boy,' that's just weird."

Silas drank from his bottle, considering Warren and who he'd spent time with the last couple of years. It was easier than thinking about the sudden kiss. "But you have had sex, right?"

Warren gave him a withering look.

"I'm just checking," Silas said, one hand up. "Chill." Confirmation was nice. The idea that Warren had built up a wealth of experience worthy of a withering look was not. "That guy you lived with first year?" he guessed.

"Straight." Warren rolled his eyes and sat back. "I'm not telling you. I don't kiss and tell."

"You already proved that," Tal pointed out. "But we're going to obsess until you throw us a bone. Who are you getting with these days?"

Warren pursed his lips, and Silas had the weirdest

sensation in his stomach. He was suddenly sure that whoever the jerk was that Warren was using for sex—or being used by, it could go either way—he wasn't anywhere near right for Silas' buddy. If he was an all right person, Warren would have come out and told them.

"I don't think," Warren said slowly, "that I'm going to tell you that. I will tell you, though, that he's a nice guy, we've been hooking up for about eight months, and we are not dating. He's out, we get along, but there's nothing really there. It's a convenience." He nodded once, clearly considering the matter closed.

"Does he go to school here and his partner is waiting for him at home, wherever that is?" Tal asked, much to Silas' relief. He certainly hadn't wanted to be the one to ask.

"You think I'd be the other man?" Warren asked with one eyebrow up. "Thanks a lot."

"You said convenience." Tal didn't seem concerned. "Can you tell me what that means?"

"It means I don't want a relationship to distract me from school, and he doesn't want a relationship to distract him from his thing. He's not a student, but I met him through a lecture. We had a meal, we flirted a bit, and then we had sex. Once in a while I'll call him, see if he's free, or he'll call me and I'll go over." Warren shrugged. "It's all we need. We have fun and then I go home until the next time. I assume he's dating other people as well. I've never asked."

Tal looked impressed. Silas wanted to kick them both. Someone was just fucking Warren and not making him feel special.

"I need another drink," Silas said, pointing to the fridge. He needed a lot more drinks. For the first time ever, Silas wanted to drink himself to unconsciousness.

"If you have more to drink, there will be problems,"

Tal said mildly. "Time for a movie and a time out, I think."

"Are you the moderator of my intervention?" Warren asked brightly. "Are there going to be questions about what kind of sex I like?"

"No," Tal said with a laugh. "I have rules the same as you guys do."

Silas drank from his beer bottle, trying to make it last. If Tal wasn't going to give him more, this was what he had to work with. "What are we watching?"

Tal shrugged and put in a disc. "*Men in Black*, of course."

It was the perfect movie for them—old, one they'd all seen a hundred times or more starting when they were kids. Warren's favorite bit was always at the beginning, when the newly-minted Agent J was taken to headquarters, and since it was his birthday they didn't make fun of him when he laughed at the funny parts just as hard as he had the first time. Tal had once tried to explain that, while the movie was funny, it wasn't slapstick, but Warren had told him that it didn't matter. Funny was funny, so shut up.

Silas liked the car chases and slime best, of course, and he made them rewind the part when the pawn shop owner got his head exploded. Tal did eventually cough up another round of drinks, so Silas sat where he was and had a nice, drunken think, head explosions aside. He'd seen the movie enough times that he could follow along without really paying attention.

He had no idea why he was so keyed up. They'd done exactly what they wanted to do—got Warren out of the closet, sort of, and found out he was no longer a virgin. That should have been the end of it, aside from now being able to hound him mercilessly about what kind of guy he was into and how soon could they fix him up with someone. But instead Silas was off kilter, completely taken by surprise by how protective he felt toward Warren.

He wondered if Warren had ever had the urge to lecture him about condoms and then thought that yes, he must have, since Warren had always been shoving them at him at weird moments. On the heels of *that* came the realization that Warren probably had bought rubbers a long time before he'd ever used them, just to make sure Silas was safe.

Smiling, he looked over at the other bed. His smile grew as he watched Warren mouth the words to his favorite scene.

Well, okay, then. He was protective. That was natural, and Warren had been protective of him, too. Cool.

Feeling better, Silas watched the movie and drank beer, pleased that he and Tal had done the right thing and that it had gone so well.

Chapter Seven

Relapse

Tal and Olivia sat together on the bench seat, looking at Warren on the other side of the table. "Slow down," Tal said quietly. "You're doing that hand wave thing. Are you okay? Like, are you hurt anywhere?"

Warren took a deep breath and wrapped his hands around his coffee mug. "I'm not damaged," he said, clearly trying to keep his voice down and his breathing calm. "I'm furious. He's going to drive me crazy, Tal. I swear, if he wasn't my best friend, I'd punch him in the mouth."

Tal blinked. "Jesus." He'd never heard Warren say anything like that about anyone, least of all Silas. He would never have thought it possible. He glanced at Olivia. "Um. Would you mind if Warren and I talk this out alone?"

"Of course not." She got up and gathered her things. "I'll see you later." She leaned over and kissed Tal, then put one of her hands on top of Warren's wrist. "It'll work out," she said softly. "Even when he's being an idiot, he does it with good intentions." She gave Warren a pat and left, waving to Tal as she opened the door to go.

"She's nice," Warren told him. "Do everything you can to make her happy."

Tal nodded. "I will. What did Silas do?"

Warren looked grim again, and his knuckles went white around his mug. "He's been coming to rehearsals all spring. Not just dropping in at the end to see if I want to get something to eat, but sitting at the back and hanging out and just lurking. He does his homework there. So I asked him a couple of weeks ago why he's suddenly doing this, and if he's babysitting me, trying to find out who I'm... uh, not dating." His gaze flicked around the cafe. "You know."

"I know." Tal nodded. He hadn't known that Silas was doing that, though. "What did he say?"

"Some crap about how he could actually work better there since his roommate's a pain and there's fewer distractions than at the library. Whatever, I didn't care much since my friend isn't connected with theater and Silas isn't going to sleuth out anything anyway. You know, I'd probably have told him by now if he wasn't being so pushy about figuring it out."

"Maybe you should just do it anyway," Tal suggested. "He just wants to know you're okay." Truthfully, Tal wanted to know, too. He wasn't crazy about anyone having a relationship based entirely on sex, no matter how many times he'd appeared totally hormonal in the past. It just didn't seem right to him, and he'd thought that Warren was the kind of guy who valued the whole package, not merely *a* package.

"My point," Warren said, ignoring the advice, "is that he's treating me like a kid all of a sudden. But I could deal with that. If nothing else, we've been hanging out more. But twice this week I caught him going through my phone, reading my text messages!" Warren looked outraged.

Tal sat back. That was pretty low, he had to admit. "Did he say anything when you caught him?"

"The first time he said he was looking through the messages from himself, looking for a phone number he sent me. He'd cleaned out his own phone and lost it." Warren drank coffee. "So it was weird and a little rude, but fine. But the second time I heard a message come in and when I came to get my phone, he was reading it. He just... picked up my phone, clicked on through, and read it."

Tal winced. He didn't even do that with Olivia's phone, ever. "Dude." A horrible thought occurred to him. "Was it from your friend?"

"No, my boss. But that's what he was looking for, I know it. And seriously, what if I do tell him? What if I tell you both or even introduce you guys? So what? What will that tell either of you? Why does it matter so much?"

Tal leaned forward, carefully moving his cup out of the way. "It matters because we care about you, Warren, you know that. But you're right—until you give the word, it's your business. You're a big boy and can do what you want. Do you want me to talk to Silas or do you just want to vent at me? Either way is good."

Warren sighed, suddenly looking tired. "I'll deal with it. And I guess I can... well, I won't have a dinner party for all of you, but I'll stop being so secretive. I think the mystery is part of what's got Silas so ramped."

"Partly." Tal nodded. "He can't stand not knowing things. I'm a little surprised he's not making you go to a lot of GSA meetings, though."

"He is. You have class that night. Wednesday."

"Ah." Tal smiled. "Is he trying to introduce you to a lot of nice boys he's picked out for you?"

"No." Warren looked thoughtful. "He's not. Is that as weird as I think it is?"

Tal pushed very hard on the idea that was taking shape at the back of his mind. "It's a little weird," he allowed. "But then, you did make kind of a big deal about not wanting a relationship while you're trying to win every academic prize ever created."

"I suppose." Warren drank more coffee, draining the mug. "He hasn't replaced Lance yet. It's been a couple of months. That's weird, and you can't even say it's only a little weird. He's fighting off guys, and you know it." Usually Silas only fought them off long enough to make sure they weren't total idiots, then he was all in.

"I noticed that." Tal's uneasy idea started to take shape. "Listen, Warren. It would be a really, really good idea if you sort of... pay attention. You know?"

Warren gave him a look of complete confusion. "I always do. My GPA, have you seen it?"

"I mean to Silas and to subtlety and to the world around you." Tal sat back. "You've been hiding for a very, very long time, and I don't want to see you trip on something. Just keep your eyes open and be careful."

Warren nodded slowly, his brow furrowed. "Okay, if you say so." His phone chirped at him and he glanced down at it. "Silas. I have to go—we're going over his first draft for his symbolism paper. Want to come?"

Tal shook his head. "I'm going to go find Olivia. Say hey for me, though. Lunch tomorrow?"

Warren got up. "Yeah. Thanks for letting me vent. I'm not going to hit him now. I might even tell him about my... about Liam. Liam McNeil, draftsman." His cheeks went faintly pink.

"Thanks." Tal smiled at him. That was more like it. Trust. "Thanks, Warren."

Warren nodded and slung his backpack over his shoulder, texting Silas as he left.

Tal sat back and thought for a moment, then called

Olivia's cell. "Baby, times are getting interesting. Where are you?" He wasn't sure if what he was seeing was good or awful. Maybe she could tell him.

Silas was crossing the space between the dining hall and their dorm when he saw Warren coming from the other direction. Since they were going to the same place—Warren's room—to go over his paper, Silas adjusted his speed so they met at the door, both of them swiping their IDs to log in.

"Have a good day?" Silas asked. Warren looked tense, he thought.

"It was all right. You?" Warren led the way up the stairs. The elevator was crap and the trip up was only three floors.

"Same." Silas followed along, wondering if Warren sounded cranky or just stressed out. Maybe he wasn't eating right or sleeping enough. That was pretty typical, since he studied so much and was always working on some project or other instead of just slapping it together at the last minute. Not that Silas did that. Much.

They got to Warren's door, and Silas waited while Warren unlocked it. The rest of the floor was pretty quiet, only a few doors propped open, and no one was playing music too loudly. "I think Kevin is working tonight, so he won't be back until ten," Warren said as they went in.

"We'll be done long before that, I hope." Silas put his bag on the bed and rummaged around for his thumb drive. "I just need help with the second section, I think."

"Okay." Warren booted his computer and took off his coat and shoes. "Want to tell me why you're acting so weird?"

"What?" Silas looked around at him.

"You." Warren took the thumb drive and sat at his desk. "You're being all weird at me, always at rehearsals even though I'm just the prop guy, checking my phone. And you're not dating anyone. Even Tal thinks that's a little weird."

Silas shrugged a shoulder. "Maybe I just thought I'd take a page from your book, you know? Buckle down, get some work done. If you don't want me at the theater, I won't go." He busied himself with his bag. He did not want to have this conversation, not at all.

"I didn't say that." Warren's voice changed. He wasn't challenging, all of a sudden, just confused. "I like it when you're there. I do."

Silas smiled at him. "Okay." Good.

Warren shook his head a tiny bit and put the thumb drive in. "Where's the doc?"

"There." Silas leaned over to watch him scroll. "Symbols." When he realized he was close enough to smell Warren's soap, he backed up. "Thanks."

With the document open, silence fell for a few minutes while Warren scanned through it, reading the ten pages quickly. Silas looked around the room, noting yet again that Warren and Kevin shared the same level of cleaning disorder: military. It was entirely possible that they had the cleanest and neatest room on the whole campus.

"Liam McNeil."

Silas turned, thinking hard. "I don't think I've read him. He wasn't on the list." Oh, crap. If he was short a source and missed something big, he was going to have to stay up half the night.

"No." Warren shook his head and turned back to the computer. "That's who... um. My friend. That's his name. He's a draftsman, not connected to the college." Silas could see that his ear was twitching, like Warren was working his jaw.

"Oh." He knew he had to say something else, but Silas was completely at a loss. Here was what he'd been looking for, and his reaction was practically nil. "Um. Okay." He sat down. "He's still being nice to you? I mean, he's not being a jerk?"

Warren gave him a quick look and then smiled. "He's fine. I mean, it's not like I just go over and we get to it, if that's what you're thinking. We talk and stuff."

"About what?" Silas wasn't sure he should be asking. He wasn't sure where the boundaries were with Warren anymore, but he was determined to find out, one way or another. Sneaking up on them wasn't working; maybe bulling through until he hit a wall would do it.

"Just stuff." Warren turned to face him, holding a pen in one hand. "I ask him how work is going, he asks about school. He doesn't know anything about my classes, really, just that I'm taking a bunch of social theory and some marketing classes. We have dinner sometimes, and talk about books or current events."

"Nothing really personal? Like, he doesn't ask after your mom or anything?"

Warren laughed. "No. Nothing like that. We're not dating, I keep telling you. He's just a guy and I'm just a guy and we get along okay. There's no spark, no connection, really. We're acquaintances with benefits, I guess."

Silas sighed. "It's working for you, so I won't say anything. It just doesn't seem like you, is all. You should be all mushy and sweet and in love and seeing hearts all over."

"I will be." Warren smiled at him. "I want to be. I do. Just not right now. For now, this is okay. No pressure, no fights, no long discussions. Just a friendly dinner and some really fun rolling around on the couch or floor or bed." He shrugged. "I like the sex."

"That's because sex is fun." Silas nodded. He was a

fan of sex, too. "How often do you see him?"

"Every couple of weeks." Warren shrugged one shoulder and rolled the pen between his palms. "Sometimes a little more, every ten days or so?"

Silas blinked. "Dude. How are you not dead of blue balls? When I have a boyfriend, I'm getting it about every two days—every day if we can find an empty room."

Warren raised an eyebrow at him. "You might want to look into this thing called 'cold showers.' I don't have that kind of time, and I'm not going to die due to lack of orgasms. I know how to jerk off, after all."

Silas snorted. "Daily ritual, man."

"The whole freaking dorm."

Silas grinned. "I've heard stories about the frats."

"Gross." Warren shuddered.

"No, no. Good stories. Hot ones."

"I really, really doubt it."

"Move over." Silas got up and pulled the other chair over to the desk. "Let me surf."

Warren snickered but moved his chair away and turned over the keyboard. "I'm not watching porn with you. Although, if it'll make you feel better, you're the only person I ever would watch porn with. But I'm not."

Silas grinned at him. "Now we're going to, someday. We'll pick a weekend when I have my room to myself, send Tal off to la la land with the lovely Olivia, and stock up on food and beer."

"And watch porn." Warren didn't sound like he was going for it. "Uh, no."

"Uh, yeah. But that day, my friend, is not today." He got online and started clicking links from a URL he knew by heart. "Here. Read this." He sat back and gave Warren what he hoped was a daring look and not a leer. He knew full well that the way to get Warren interested in anything was to include documentation.

Warren rolled his eyes and, looking entirely like he was only reading in order to do Silas a big favor, started to read. "This is so dumb. Look at the spelling."

"Look past the spelling to the hot," Silas coaxed. "The hand jobs. The blow jobs. The licking and kissing and dirty talk."

"For the love of God, I can't believe I'm reading this stuff." Warren read silently for a moment and then his eyes widened slightly. "Oh."

"Uh-huh." Silas grinned and watched Warren's face. "Keep going."

"Maybe we should be working on your paper."

"We will. Right after you read that to the end." Silas pointed at the computer screen. "One story, save the link, and then we'll do my paper. Okay?"

Warren made a sound of frustration that Silas ignored—he'd been hearing that sound for years and it meant he was winning. He sat back and let Warren read, unabashedly watching Warren's face for reactions.

"Stop staring at me," Warren told him, not looking away from the screen.

"Aw." Silas rolled his eyes and made a show of looking at the ceiling. "Are you blushing?"

"Do you want me to help with your paper at all? Because I can toss you out and just read porn, it's all the same to me."

Silas shut up. After about thirty seconds of silence, he risked sneaking a peak. Warren was reading still, his eyes darting back and forth as he appeared to devour the rather scanty storyline. Years of observation let Silas know that he really was reading, his attention totally caught. Warren's lips were very slightly parted and his eyebrows were showing his reactions as they either drew together in a slight frown or shot up as he read something that intrigued him.

The eyebrows were up a lot.

Silas smiled, watching Warren scroll down through the screen. He hadn't expected anything dramatic like Warren starting to pant or lick his lips or rub his crotch or anything, but he could follow the subtlety of Warren's eyebrows better than any overt cues someone else might need. He also felt rather pleased that his first effort at finding Warren's taste in erotica had been somewhat of a success. Frat boys. Who knew?

"Okay, enough of that." Warren clicked something in his browser and added a bookmark. "This doesn't mean we're going to go for dinner and talk about hot guys, does it?"

"Totally." Silas nodded seriously. "We're gonna rock the beach this summer, too."

Warren snorted. "Have you ever seen me at a beach? Ever?"

"Fine, we'll rock the literary festival." Silas waved a hand. "And after midterms, you and I are going to make a weekend of just eating bad food, watching movies and porn, and planning for summer. Last summer sucked."

Warren nodded and then shrugged one shoulder. "I had steady hours, but you're right. We were too busy to spend any time together. And then there was Jaymes."

"Yeah. Sorry." Silas winced. Jaymes hadn't been in his life long, but it had been long enough that Jaymes'd had time to insult Warren for being smart, piss off Tal for being Tal, and even get Silas' mother to ask what exactly his problem was. Silas still wasn't sure what had made Jaymes so irresistible, since he was only moderately good looking and average in most other ways, including his talents in bed. "At least I got rid of him before the end of July."

"True. And we thank you for it." Warren pulled up Silas' paper and scrolled to the section that needed work.

"I was really mad at you, earlier," he said. "I talked to Tal about it."

Silas made a face. He knew he shouldn't have picked up Warren's phone. "Did it help?"

"Yeah." Warren looked at him. "I'm sorry I've been so willfully secretive. But I'm scared that you'll be taking over my whole life now that I've told you. I don't want to date, Silas. I don't want to be sucked into that whole world yet. Can you give me space?"

"I can," Silas told him, holding in a sigh. "I promise, I can. I'll back off. Thank you for telling me his name. I swear to God I won't try to meet him or anything. I won't even Google him."

Warren smiled a little. "Don't make promises you won't be able to keep."

"Well, okay." Silas appreciated that Warren knew he was trying, even if that last bit had been a stretch. "I might Google him. But I won't do anything else. Will you tell me when you go over there, though, so I know to tell the cops if you don't come back?" He squealed and tried to jump out of the way, laughing as Warren made a grab for him. "Kidding!"

"That is so not funny." Warren was laughing, though, and still trying to either whap him or wrestle Silas out of the chair, it was hard to tell which. "And just for that, I'm going to lay a false trail—tell you I'm going over there and sneak off to the library to get some work done."

"You really do live your life on the edge." Silas grinned at him and pushed back until Warren fell away, back in front of the computer. "Are you going to help me with this paper or not?"

"Yeah, yeah. You owe me."

"Put it on my tab." Silas moved his chair closer, feeling more relaxed and at ease than he had in more than a month. Things were going to be okay. Warren was still

Warren, and they were back on track. "I've got some DVDs you can borrow." They could share porn, finally. That was cool.

Warren just rolled his eyes and started pointing out where Silas needed more structure in his paper.

Normalcy had been achieved.

"Well, it's good that you told them." Liam sat across from him and ate a mouthful of pasta. "Don't you feel better? A little?"

"I guess." Warren, done with his meal, was sitting back and drinking water from a tall glass. "Well, yes, of course. They're my best friends; it feels good to tell them most everything. They don't judge. They just worry." He rolled his eyes. "I think the worst of that is over."

"Both of them?" Liam pushed his dark hair out of his eyes and looked intently at Warren's face.

"Uh-huh. Tal's just quieter about it than Silas. But he's also the one who just lays it out, no bullshit. Silas tries to, but he's more..." Warren waved a hand in a roller-coaster motion. "He feels thing pretty big and he's very enthusiastic. Tal spends more time thinking things over and coming up with the exact words he wants to say."

Liam nodded. "That can be good. Both ways. They kind of have a balance, then?"

"More or less," Warren agreed. "And now that they both know for sure that I'm gay, and they both know about you and I've laid my boundaries out for them, things are quiet. I think Silas will even start to date again. He wasn't waiting for me, by any means, but I think he was trying to keep his time free, just in case I needed his help with some big gay crisis."

Liam laughed, which was good, and finished his

supper, which was better. "They sound like they're good friends for you to have." He got up and took both their plates to the sink. "How's school going?"

"Good." Warren got up, too. "How's work?"

"Good." Liam smiled and drew Warren to him, kissing him lightly on the mouth and letting one hand drop to Warren's ass for a quick pat. They were almost exactly the same height, so everything lined up nicely, which came in handy in many ways. "I got a couple of movies in the mail; do you have time to stay for one?"

Warren considered that. He had a paper to hand in the next afternoon, but it was all done, only in need of one read-through and printing. He had reading to do, as well, but he could do that in a couple of hours. "I have to leave by nine."

"Good enough." Liam took his hand and led him to the living room. "We'll put it in and see if it's worth paying attention."

"It's got some competition." Warren held Liam's hand a little tighter, giving it a squeeze. "Frankly, it'll have to be pretty great to grab me."

"Well, then." Liam smiled and kissed him again, this time licking through Warren's mouth and pressing their bodies close together. "That's what I like to hear."

"I like to hear the sounds you make," Warren said without a trace of embarrassment or shyness. They'd done this often enough to know that they liked the same things, that they were both going to have a good time. He put one hand flat on the small of Liam's back and pushed it down, over his ass. "Put the movie in, though. Who knows, it might be okay."

Liam did so, not wasting any time. "You're wound up." They usually at least let dinner settle.

"Do you mind?" Warren was still standing next to the couch.

"Hell, no." The disc started up, and Liam navigated his way through the menus to start the movie. "I don't mind at all." He gestured to the end table, which had a drawer. "All stocked up."

"Awesome." Warren moved and got out a couple condoms. "Sit."

"Sit?" Liam gave him a long, slow smile.

"Take off your pants and sit," Warren amended. He opened one of the rubbers and watched as Liam complied. Liam was a little thicker than he was—shoulders, chest, hips—but Warren liked that. Warren had found that he liked rather a lot about Liam's body in the time they'd spent together, and he was comfortable navigating his way around and over it. "You banged your hip again." A small bruise on Liam's hipbone was testament to the fact that Liam's drafting desk was still too close to his office door.

"I wouldn't be complete without a little ache there," Liam said. He rubbed the bruise and then his mostly hard cock, bringing it to full hardness before sitting on the couch and leaning back. "You're still dressed."

Warren looked down at his jeans and long-sleeved T. "Yup." Staying that way, he went to his knees between Liam's thighs and rolled the rubber on.

"Nice." Liam laughed softly and ran his fingers through Warren's hair. "You got it cut."

"Just a little." A trim was necessary sometimes, or he'd be forever blowing it out of his eyes. "Watch the movie." Warren hadn't even checked to see what it was. He didn't care—this was what he wanted. He lowered his head and rubbed his cheek on the soft skin of Liam's thigh, then nuzzled at Liam's balls.

"Come on," Liam whispered. "You're teasing."

Warren didn't say anything at all, just nuzzled again, one hand stroking Liam's cock lazily. He hated the taste of the junk on the condoms, so he usually tried to get most of it off first. He waited until Liam's hand tried to make a fist in his hair before licking anything, and he started with Liam's nuts.

With one of the soft groans Warren loved to hear, Liam spread his legs wider, and his cock gave a little jump in Warren's hand.

When Warren got Liam's balls wet, he sucked one into his mouth, groaning himself when Liam gasped and hitched his hips forward, trying to grind into Warren's face. He squeezed Liam's cock and released his nut, suddenly wanting to suck Liam's cock more than anything.

Liam fed it to him, one hand on the back of Warren's head, which was something Warren usually disliked. But this time he was hungry enough to let it go, and he didn't mind at all when Liam drew him down, his hips lifting. Warren just put his hands on Liam's thighs and went with it, sucking hard and letting Liam thrust right into his throat. If Liam pushed too hard, or if the hand pulling his face down into Liam's crotch was too much, he just dug in with his nails. Liam got the point.

They were both breathing hard, Warren through his nose and Liam panting out curses and praise. The cock in Warren's mouth was hard and unyielding, so stiff he couldn't find softness anywhere, and under his tongue he could almost feel the blood moving through thick veins. Liam pried one of Warren's hands from his leg and pulled it to his balls.

Warren laughed, his mouth full, and looked up Liam's body to see him with his head tipped back, Liam looking at the ceiling as he moaned. Warren kept watching, his hand rolling the tight balls and his tongue scrubbing at the spot under the ridge of Liam's glans.

"Oh, fuck, yes." Liam was whispering to the room, and behind them the movie wasn't even background noise, just an irritating hum. "No, stop. I'm gonna come. Too soon."

Warren shook his head and dropped his hand to rub over Liam's hole.

"Oh, shit." Liam's stomach clenched and he curled up as he came, filling the condom in rapid bursts. "Fuck me."

Warren held Liam in his mouth until Liam had stopped shooting, then stood up to get out of his clothes as quickly as he could, leaving Liam to deal with the used rubber. He toed off his shoes as he peeled off the shirt, then had his jeans down and off before Liam had really gotten himself cleaned up. He grabbed the other rubber and tore the wrapper open, watching as Liam sprawled for him, one foot on the floor and one on the couch. Liam's cock had barely softened, and was still mostly hard, his skin flushed.

"Come on, then," Liam invited as Warren got the rubber on. "Grab the lube, you're closer. And can walk."

"Weak in the knees?" Warren got it from the drawer and put too much in his palm. This was going to be sloppy.

"You know it. You're all worked up tonight."

Warren shrugged and got his dick slick, then used the rest on Liam's ass. He worked a couple of fingers in, kneeling on the couch and looking down, watching. He loved watching this, he'd found out. His fingers sinking in, his cock sliding and thrusting, it was all a huge turn on. He'd never managed to watch when Liam fucked him, but when he was doing this, he couldn't seem to stop himself from looking.

"That's it," Liam encouraged. "There." His body gave way and he made more noises, apparently as into it as Warren was, despite already getting off. He stroked himself slowly. "Right there."

Warren nodded, his fingers rubbing. His cock was a hot, aching thing, but he wanted to wait until Liam was revved back up. "Can you take more?" he asked, wanting to get three fingers in, wanting to open Liam up wide.

"Yeah, do it." Liam lifted the foot he had on the couch up and put his leg over Warren's shoulder. "Do what you want."

Warren glanced up at him, startled.

"Anything. Fuck me hard, hold me down, flip me over. Whatever." Liam tugged at his cock faster, his breathing picking up again. "Do what you want to, Warren. Just make sure you get your cock in my ass before I come again."

Warren narrowed his eyes. His balls were starting to ache. "Shh." He shoved three fingers in.

"Yes!" Liam arched, his hand holding his balls. "Do it."

His own breathing growing ragged, Warren fingered him for a moment, hand sawing in and out. The lube was getting tacky. "Liam. Look at me."

Liam looked. Warren pulled his fingers out, then slammed his cock home, going deep, one hand on the couch for balance.

Liam arched again, driving his hips up, his ass clinging.

"Shit," Warren hissed. He closed his eyes and stayed where he was, fighting for control, his heart pounding and his ears filled with the roar of his breathing.

"Do it," Liam insisted in a harsh whisper.

Warren pulled out, stood up, grabbed Liam by the hips, and flipped him over. Ass high, body draped awkwardly over the couch, Warren took him again, fucking Liam's ass with rapid thrusts. He could barely make sense of the words he was hearing, Liam telling him harder, or faster, or oh God, yes, but his body knew what it was doing. Over and over he pounded in, noticing when Liam reached under himself to jack off, and then hearing the warning pitch in Liam's gasp.

Warren thrust deep and felt Liam coming around him, felt the grasp and pull and flutter of his muscles. He wanted to come so badly, wanted to shoot and release and collapse onto Liam's back, wanted the high of orgasm.

And yet, there he was, almost in pain, his balls high and hot and his cock aching.

He suddenly heard a voice in his head. "We'll watch porn together." Warren let go and came in a rapid shotgun of jerks, his whole world exploding with the shock of it.

Chapter Eight

Breaking Ground

Midterms came and went, and Silas fell into his bed for almost thirty-six hours. He got up long enough to shower, eat, check in with Tal to make sure it was Thursday and not Friday, and then went back to sleep. He woke up again when Warren arrived with chicken soup and deep fried wontons for him, which were clearly an excuse to make sure Silas wasn't actually sick.

"You shouldn't worry by now," Silas told him, a thermometer in his mouth to prove he was okay. "After three years of college and six sets of midterms, I'd think you'd be used to this."

"The rest of us don't sleep round the clock as soon as our last test is done," Warren pointed out. "And you don't do it after finals, just midterms." He checked the thermometer, nodded once, and added, "See you tomorrow morning?"

Silas was already crawling back into his bed. "Yeah, come by around eleven. Turn out the light when you go." And then he was asleep again, his body shutting down and rebooting.

The next thing he knew, he was wide awake, the sun was shining in, and he was absolutely starving. He ate the greasy wontons and cold chicken soup while he gathered his things for the shower and then headed down the hall, wondering what time his roommate had left; the whole dorm was still quiet, most people still sleeping, but the other bed had been empty. Maybe Kevin just hadn't come in the night before.

Showered, awake, and still hungry, Silas got back to his room to dress and saw the note stuck on his laptop. "Gone home for weekend, back Sunday night. Didn't know if you wanted booze for weekend, only got a six pack for the fridge. If you drink it, you owe me."

Silas grinned and got dressed. It was going to be a good weekend.

In the dining hall, he had a table to himself as he downed enough breakfast for two people. It wasn't quite eight o'clock on a Friday morning without any classes, so the people who had stayed on campus for the weekend were mostly sleeping late, he assumed. It was too early to text or call Warren or Tal, so Silas went back to his room and got his laundry together. He could have all his chores done by noon, leaving the weekend blessedly free, other than some reading for Monday's classes.

Energized, cheerful, Silas cleaned up the room in between trips up and down the stairs to the washing machine. He went through his binders and got his notes put back where they belonged after studying for midterms, and then he swept the floor clear of pieces of paper and the weird things that accumulated in the corners.

"You're chipper." Warren leaned on the frame of his door, his hands in his jeans pockets. "Slept well?"

Silas grinned at him and put the last of the books back on the shelf. "Yep. And had a huge breakfast, did the laundry, and cleaned up. Roommate is gone for the

113

weekend, and the sun is shining. Let's grab Tal and go bike riding or something. Hiking. Climbing. Touch football. Something."

"Jesus." Warren shook his head. "It's a good thing you don't sleep around the clock more than twice a year. Come on, I need to eat. You can keep me company."

"Breakfast is over." Silas grabbed his keys and his phone, though. "Did you just get up?"

"No, an hour or so ago. Come on, I want muffins. We can go to Cafe Sol."

Silas knew it would be slammed there, but that was okay. They could get food to go and just walk around for a while. He sent a text to Tal telling him where they'd be, and they left the dorm. People were up and moving by then, and it seemed that most people shared Silas' enthusiasm for the sun—every bench was occupied, and most steps to buildings had one or two people sitting outside chatting or reading or just basking like cats.

"I love spring," Silas declared. He felt like he could move mountains.

"And sleep. You love sleep and spring." Warren smiled at him. "I'm surprised you're not chasing down some pretty guy and sowing a few oats, the mood you're in."

Silas shrugged. "Maybe later. It's a long weekend."

"You'll get to it, I'm sure." Warren turned his face to the sun. "How about that guy who came into the meeting late last time? The one in the green shirt. He seemed friendly."

"Yeah, he was cute, but he was there to pick up his boyfriend."

"Really?" Warren blinked at him. "Huh. Totally missed that."

"I know, you were too busy talking to the baby dyke. How is she, by the way?"

"Freaked. I think she'll be okay, though. It was her

first time being ditched for a guy, and that's gotta suck."

Silas nodded. He'd had a couple of guys date him and then go out with girls again. It was a very weird feeling to watch that, but it happened a lot at college. "I did ask Peter to have coffee with me next week, though. He said yes, but that he'd have to get back to me about a time— he's got labs."

"He's nice," Warren said vaguely. "Let me know how it goes. God, look at that line. Wait here, no sense in us both going in. Want anything?"

Silas asked for a bacon and cheese scone and went to sit on a bench next to the cafe. It would take Warren a few minutes to get through the line and back out. He texted Tal again while he waited, and got one back from Olivia that simply read, "Busy." Silas grinned and put his phone away.

By the time Warren came back out, Silas had made a plan for them. All he needed was for Warren to go along with it until his resistance was totally gone, and since he was feeling so energetic, Silas thought he stood a pretty good chance. "Do you have plans for this weekend?" he asked, taking the scone Warren handed him. "Any dates with Liam or meetings with study groups?"

"Sunday afternoon, but other than that, no." Warren looked at him warily. "You look dangerous."

"It's just my Friday face; relax. Want to go downtown today? I'll even go to the bookstores with you, as long as you come to the music store with me. Tal and Olivia seem pretty tied up right now, but maybe they can meet us for supper."

Warren nodded. "Yeah, okay. Bus or bikes?"

"Bikes." It was far too nice a day for the bus, and riding their bikes meant that Warren would keep his book buying down to only ten or so that he could fit in his backpack.

"Sure." They started walking again, back toward the dorms. "Movies tonight? I have my room to myself."

"So do I. And I have beer in the fridge." Six would do the two of them fine. If Tal came along there would even be enough for him, but Tal didn't really fit into the Gay-Porn-With-Warren portion of the plan. Silas had faith in Olivia, though; he figured they wouldn't see a whole lot of Tal until Sunday.

"Your place, then," Warren agreed. "I'll bring food or something. I think I have some chips."

"Fabulous." Silas loved it when a plan came together.

Warren was beginning to suspect he'd been set up, but he couldn't figure out how or why. Or even why it was a bad thing. He was doing exactly what he would have wanted to do with a totally free day, and somehow it felt carefully constructed.

He'd had his muffin—a huge and beautiful concoction of banana and chocolate—and a great ride downtown on his bike. Silas was right, the weather was perfect for getting out of the stale air of dorm rooms and classrooms. They'd wandered around for a while, and Tal had met up with them in the early afternoon, the three of them bouncing from bookstore to music shop to thrift shops and back again with no real design. They'd had sandwiches when they were hungry, talked about everything they wanted to, and then they rode back to the campus together in time for Tal to go find Olivia for the evening.

"She wants me to meet her family in a couple weeks," Tal said with a grimace. "I have no idea if that's as big a deal as I think it is, but it feels pretty huge."

"It is," Silas and Warren said together. "Don't blow it."

"Thanks." Tal rolled his eyes and left them at the bike rack. "I'll see you tomorrow—we're going to a movie later on, and she said something about meeting Karen and Lori for dancing."

"Have fun." Warren waved, and they watched Tal go to the doors closest to his room. "He better not screw up. I like Olivia."

Silas laughed and nodded. "I don't think he will. He likes her even more than we do."

"So, what's next?" Warren hefted his backpack. "I need to go unpack this, first thing." He had five new books, and two of them were pure whimsy.

"I'm coming with you," Silas said with one eyebrow high. "Just to make sure you don't start reading. Want to go to the dining hall for supper or grab some take-out?"

"Dining hall. My meal card has more money on it than my wallet has in it."

"Good enough."

By the time they'd left the books in Warren's room, walked to the dining hall and eaten, and walked back to Warren's room to grab the snacks for later, Warren was ready to sit for a while. Silas might still be full of energy, but Warren was thinking of a nap. He was considering bailing on the movie watching, but Silas swept him along, talking nonstop about nothing in particular, and before Warren could figure out if he really wanted to call it a day or not, he was already back in Silas' room, flopped on his bed.

"How do you do this?" he asked, watching Silas flip through a stack of DVDs.

"I move my fingers like this, and the discs flop over." Silas looked at him. "Do what?"

"I don't know." He really didn't. "Never mind. What are we watching?"

Silas shrugged. "What are you in the mood for?

Explosions, funny stuff, sexy stuff, or science fiction?"

"Science fiction." That was easy. "With explosions."

"Naturally." Silas grinned and put a movie in his computer. "Can you see?"

Warren nodded and moved over on the bed to make room. He'd brought his pillows, so there were plenty to go around without having to lift any from the other bed. "Don't let me fall asleep."

"I won't." Silas brought them each a beer and got comfortable next to him, then got up again to turn up the volume a little and make sure the door was locked. Warren didn't raise an eyebrow at that—Friday night in the men's dorm, it was just smart to make sure your door was locked or you'd wind up with a party in your room without ever wanting one.

The title sequence started up and Warren said, "Oh, I've never seen this," which got an immediate stare from Silas.

"What do you mean you've never seen it? It's *The Matrix*, you must have seen it. Even my mom's seen it."

Warren shook his head. "Keanu Reeves is odd looking and the concept is creepy. But I'll watch it now."

"Damn right you will. Honestly, never seen *The Matrix*. That's just not right." Silas settled down again and apparently did his very best not to point things out as they watched or talk his way through it. Warren appreciated all the effort he was putting into not telling Warren all the cool things he was seeing anyway.

They both had beer while they watched, uncharacteristically finishing all six of them, and when the credits rolled, Warren was a little surprised to find himself slightly tipsy.

"Now, tell me you think that was pretty damn cool," Silas said, getting up to take the disc out. "I'll call you a liar if you don't."

Warren nodded, staying where he was and feeling a chill on his side from the loss of Silas' body heat. "It was cool," he agreed. It was. Keanu Reeves still looked odd, though. "Got another movie?" He didn't have a pressing need for sleep any longer.

"Yeah, sure." Silas didn't put in another disc, though. He clicked through files on his computer and then came back to the bed, grinning. "Move over."

"I didn't move," Warren protested. He stayed where he was and let Silas cozy up. "What are we watching?"

Silas gave him a wicked grin, the one that always reminded Warren of a flashing sign blaring "Danger! Run Away Now!"

"Oh, no." Warren looked at the computer. "Ohh, no."

"Oh, yes. Shh." Silas wiggled closer, and Warren was suddenly ready to flee. He must have telegraphed his intention, because Silas pinned him down. "You're staying. You're watching."

Warren blinked up at him, feeling both warm and fuzzy from the beer and a lot like this was a horrible idea. "If we're watching porn, you're getting off me."

Silas giggled and leered, not moving. "What?"

"Off *of* me," Warren said, stressing the second word. "Not off on me."

"Ah." Silas laughed and rolled to the side. "Okay, I'm not on you and I'm not getting off, currently. Hush now and watch the nice porn."

"It's nice porn? I had no idea there was such a thing. Isn't that an oxymoron?"

Silas snorted at him and poked him in the side. "You're a moron. Shut up and watch the boys."

Warren sighed. Maybe he'd be able to sleep through parts of the porn. That would teach Silas a lesson. What lesson, exactly, Warren wasn't sure. His evening had taken a turn for the strange. "How many times have you seen this one?"

"I dunno. Not a lot—I get bored and delete them after a few views. If they're bad, I don't even watch all the way through."

Warren turned his head to look at Silas. He hadn't seen anything on the screen yet that caught his attention—just three guys stripping off and kissing on a couch. He knew the formula—there would be blow jobs for a while before they moved on to other things. "What's your definition of bad?"

"You know, the ones with really big muscle guys with mustaches and too much dialogue. I don't mind a semblance of a story, but when they try to act, it just gets me laughing. Oh, and I don't like most of the music— this one is good 'cause you can hear them kissing and moaning and stuff. I like that. Why, what do you call bad?"

Warren noted that it was interesting they were discussing what they didn't like as opposed to what turned them on, then filed it and answered the question. "I don't generally like porn at all," he said, trying not to sound like a snob of some kind. "I find it all vaguely ridiculous. But I turn it off when it's a cast of thousands or if there's humiliation. I'll watch this kind of thing, though. Even if they do look even younger than us."

"Humiliation?" Silas looked at him, both eyebrows up. "What kind of stuff are you searching for, dude? Or what's Liam got in his collection?" The eyebrows wiggled.

"Leave him out of it." Warren looked at the computer, which was easier than looking at Silas right then. "It's the Internet. Half the time you're looking for one thing and you find another, you know that."

"Sure." Silas nodded, but laughed at him, just a little. Warren could feel the bed move ever so slightly with it. "I know. I once wound up reading about penguins half the night because I clicked one thing and then another, and before you know it... penguins."

"Stop being such a liar." Warren rolled his eyes. On the screen, two of the boys—he could hardly bring himself to call them men when they were clearly only about nineteen or so—were getting sucked off by the third. He hadn't quite worked himself up to the point where he'd take them both at once, but it was heading that way. The two guys getting licked and tugged and sucked were kissing each other and then looking down at their dicks. "So. Now we've watched porn. Time for another sci-fi?"

Silas snorted at him. "Not a chance. Shut up and watch the pretty."

Warren didn't sigh. He did roll his eyes and lie there, wondering how his life had gotten so weird. "Straight guys don't lie around watching—" He stopped, because yes, they did. He lived in a men's dorm with a couple hundred guys, most of whom were straight. They most definitely sat around and watched porn together.

"See?" Silas was laughing for sure, then. "Honestly, is it so bad?"

"No, I guess not." Warren watched for a few moments, giving himself bonus points when the guy on his knees stuffed both cocks into his mouth. "I just wish that things weren't so predictable."

"The trouble is, unpredictable is often the same as 'horrifying' and 'scary,' though." Silas sounded like he knew what he was talking about.

"Is this a full-length one or just a clip?" Warren couldn't see any progress bar from where he was.

"Are you talking so much because you're nervous?"

"Probably. Usually I'm alone when I'm watching this stuff."

"Relax, it's me." Silas gave Warren's leg a quick pat, sending shocks right through him. "Shut up and watch."

Warren shut up, because talking was suddenly a very

bad idea. He hadn't been at all into it, and mostly still wasn't, but the combination of visuals and touch had instantly changed the way his blood was flowing, and a strange situation had suddenly become a danger situation. He lay still, wishing he'd been smart enough to think ahead to how to cover up if this very thing happened.

He hadn't felt so ill-prepared or exposed in his entire life. He couldn't even twitch for fear of bringing Silas attention back to him from the screen. All he could do was watch and try to breathe properly while willing his cock to soften.

The cocksucker was on all fours, taking a prick in his mouth and having his ass played with. That wasn't going to help the situation at all. Warren closed his eyes, but he could still hear. Silas was right—they were vocal, and the music soundtrack was low enough to let every gasp and groan and wet sound of licking come right to him.

"Watch this," Silas said, his voice oddly quiet, just above a whisper. "I love this part."

Warren opened his eyes, unable to resist. He could barely make out the words the actors were saying—the real dialogue had been looped, but this apparently wasn't in the script and was therefore unimportant.

"Ready?" the one behind was asking, rubbing his cock over the middle one's hole. He nudged his knees further apart.

"Uh-huh." No sucking going on now, just waiting.

Then penetration—slow and long, and the camera caught the curve of backs and the way their faces changed, both of them sighing and closing their eyes at the same time.

It was intimate, and for a moment Warren couldn't breathe. It was possibly the most real thing he'd seen on film, ever, and he had a flash of embarrassment for intruding.

"See?" Silas did whisper then. "It gets me every time. That's why I still have this one."

Warren looked at him without meaning to. Silas' face was slightly flushed, just a little bit of color that most people would have missed. "Yeah," he said, and his voice was far too raspy. He looked away again, fast, wishing he hadn't said anything.

Silas moved on the bed, far too close. "Warren."

"No." Impossible to avoid looking at Silas, Warren braced himself for the inevitable. "This is a very bad idea, Silas." The worst possible idea.

"It's just me." Silas touched Warren's cheek, which was somehow more profoundly *intimate* than touching his prick would have been.

Warren jerked back. "Because it's you. Bad, bad idea."

Silas, to his credit, didn't try to touch him again. "Who knows you better than I do?"

"No one. Which is my point." Warren sat up but didn't try to leave. "You're not just my friend, you're my very best friend. I don't trust anyone as much as I trust you, I don't love anyone the way I love you. Tal is close, so close you're almost an even match, but you're not. You have so much of me, Silas. You can't have this, though." He shook his head. "Not this way."

He hadn't meant to say that last part, but it was, perhaps, the most important thing he'd ever spoken.

Silas looked at him, his head tilted to the side a tiny bit. He was thinking hard, Warren knew. He could see it in Silas' eyes.

"Why not?" he finally asked, and Warren was sure that it wasn't what he'd planned to ask. He looked a little surprised with himself.

Warren gave him a sad smile, and he did stand up then, almost having to crawl over Silas' legs to get to the floor at the end of the bed. "Because you get everything you want so easily. Because you can have anyone, anytime, and do. Because I won't be just that for you, and it won't be just that one time. Not for us. And not now, in any case."

Silas pursed his lips, and his brows drew together as he thought something through. Warren put on his shoes while Silas made his way through the information and then waited, giving Silas a chance to say what he needed to say.

"I do love you, you know," Silas told him. He didn't get off the bed. "I wouldn't use you."

"I know." Warren nodded. "But I need you to be far, far more serious about this, and I'm not ready for that any more than you are. Now is not the time for us, Silas. You really should ask Peter out, though. He likes you, and he seems nice. You'll have fun."

Looking confused and thoughtful, Silas didn't move as Warren went to the door and unlocked it. He didn't say anything as Warren left, either, and Warren was reasonably sure that the whole thing would never be mentioned again.

He sincerely hoped not, anyway. He had far more to achieve before he devoted himself to dealing with Silas' place in his life. That was going to be a full-time job when it came time.

Chapter Nine

A New Sun Shines

Silas didn't officially have the use of his mother's car for the summer, but it somehow worked out that way, between their work schedules. He dropped her off at her office, went to one of his jobs in the morning and then his volunteer gig in the afternoon, picked her up and did errands like groceries, and then went to do an evening shift at his other job. She had the weekends off, and Silas was usually with Tal—who had a car of his own for the summer, thanks to his dad—or Warren, who preferred walking if they could.

But this was different. This was huge and important and all night, so he had to actually ask her for the car, like when he was seventeen. She laughed at him and shook her head. "I'm not sure I like the idea of you driving when you're this wound up. Did you have a lot of coffee today?"

Silas tried to be still but couldn't. "Just one," he said, raising his hand as if swearing a pledge. "So is it all right?"

"Since you already have the tickets, I can hardly say no." She kissed his cheek and waved him off to the door. "I release you. Have fun. See you tomorrow."

Silas boogied on out the door and over to Tal's place, hoping to get there before Warren left. They'd had the afternoon off, and as far as Silas knew they'd still be there, helping to clear a tree that had come down rather dramatically the week before.

He pulled in, pleased to see them sitting on the front steps, looking dirty but otherwise fine. They waved as he parked, and stayed where they were while he got out and bounded over to them, already talking.

"We are heading out tonight," Silas said, still wiggling around like he had something in his pants. A ferret, maybe. It didn't feel like a ferret, but it was more than ants. "Man, I can't believe I got these tickets. We're going to have a blast. The only way it could be better is if Olivia and Peter were here." He launched into the story of how he'd managed to score three tickets for the biggest concert event the city had ever hosted, which had been sold out for weeks.

Tal grinned and nodded slowly. He had a dirt smudge on his cheek that he kept rubbing at—it looked like sap, dark and sticky. "It'll be good. Total score, Silas." He leaned back and turned his pleased look toward Warren. "Good end to the day, and we don't have to drive. Nice."

"I can't go," Warren said calmly. He stood up and brushed dirt off his jeans. "I have a date, sorry."

Silas felt his jaw drop open, but couldn't seem to make himself close his mouth. Not for an instant did he doubt what Warren said, not with that tone of voice. Still, Warren didn't date. The whole idea was perfectly ridiculous. Warren had made a very big deal about how he had better things to do with his time.

Silas turned to look at Tal and then back at Warren. "With who?" he asked. He was pleased he sounded so calm.

Warren picked up a glass of water that had been on

the step above him and, still looking insufferably calm, said, "Jordan Gloss."

Silas' mouth snapped shut with a click. That couldn't be right. It mustn't be right. Jordan Gloss was the owner of a new bookstore specializing in collectables. He was a few years older than them, close to thirty.

Tal, who hadn't even moved, nodded slowly. "That's cool," he said. "Jordan's a nice guy. He's got ambition, and he's not lazy."

"I know." Warren nodded. "That's why I said yes. He's been... " His cheeks went pink and Silas blinked. Warren blushing? "He's been asking for a while." The pink grew deeper and Warren's chin came up, his look defiant. "He's been very kind and made an effort."

Tal smiled, then his gaze flicked at Silas. Silas stared at him and Tal's eyebrows shot up. "Something choking you?"

"No," Silas said quickly. This was dangerous ground all of a sudden. "Um, not bringing up things that should stay at school, but what about Liam?"

Warren shrugged one shoulder. "He's not here, I wasn't dating him, and I didn't seen him in the last month of the semester anyway. I think he's seeing someone. Besides..." He suddenly looked uncomfortable, and given the size of the bomb he'd dropped with utter calm, Silas was even more off balance, waiting. "The three of us," Warren said carefully, "need to have lunch soon. I need to tell you both about something that may or may not happen. It's good, in the long run, but it'll change things."

Tal looked up at him. "You can't do that, you know. Act all vague and mysterious. We'll sit on you and not let you up for your date."

Warren made a face and Tal actually stood up. "Okay, okay!" Warren raised both his hands. "This isn't how I wanted to tell you, is all." He took a breath. "There's a chance, better than fifty-fifty but by no means for sure, that I'm going to graduate early, at Christmas. And I'll be moving to California. My dean sent some of my work off to his mentor at one of the schools out there, a great school, and there's some interest. They really like the stuff I've been working on with social media economics. They're talking about me starting a master's program at midyear and making up some class time to finish in a year and a half. I'd have to promise to finish my PhD with them, too, but there's a lot of money involved, and it could be really good. It would mean staying out there, though, and working through the summer next year and the year after."

Silas sat on the grass. "They can do that?" He'd had no idea such a thing was even possible.

"Not really. Well, yes." Warren corrected himself. "I've done almost all my course work, just have to take two extra classes, and they can let me start whenever they want." He sighed and sat down next to Silas. "It'll be a lot of work. A lot of people are looking at me, and it'll be like letting down a lot of important people in my field if I don't give it my best shot. On a personal level, the only real thing that will change is that you two won't be with me. And Olivia," he added with a small smile. "And to be honest, that part sucks. It's scary."

Silas opened his mouth to say that he and Tal would go with him, but both Warren and Tal were shaking their heads at him. "You can't." Warren said quietly. "Too much money, too far away. I appreciate it, though, and wish you could. I know you would."

Silas nodded, suddenly miserable. "When will you know? What school?"

"Not until August. I'll tell you what school when it happens." He shrugged one shoulder. "I don't want to jinx it, honestly. All my work is under review, and the funding will have to be in place. Really, I kind of expect that it'll all fall through at the last minute. I'm still applying for my dorm room, and requesting a single, which I won't get if I'm slated to graduate early. I'm going on the assumption that I'll be right there come January."

Silas nodded and looked at Tal. Tal looked back, his face serious. "No sense getting all upset yet," Tal said to him.

"Right," Warren agreed. He stood up. "I have to go and get ready for dinner. Have a good time tonight, guys. Call me tomorrow and we'll get together. I want to hear all about it."

Tal nodded. "Will do. Have a good time with Jordan. We'll want to hear all about that."

Silas watched as Warren walked down the drive and headed toward his mother's house. He wasn't sure he wanted to hear about any of it. Not Jordan, not Warren leaving for the coast, nothing. That wasn't the way things were supposed to go.

He narrowed his eyes. He hadn't realized there was a way things were supposed to go, but there it was. This wasn't it. So, for it to be right, clearly he was supposed to be near Warren. With no Jordan. He looked at Tal, who was calmly looking back.

"I think I'm in trouble."

"I think you are, too." Tal nodded. Then he smiled. "But on the plus side, my money is on him waiting for you. He's waited this long, after all."

Silas stared at him. "I have no idea what you're talking about."

"I know." Tal laughed. "That's what makes it all marvelous. Come on. We have a concert to go to. One step at a time, my friend. One step at a time."

Silas stayed where he was. "I don't even know what the first step is. Is there a support group for this? Are there twelve steps and literature?"

Tal pulled him up to his feet and steered him into the house. "How many GSA groups have you started, run, or volunteered at? And how many people have you listened to? You've never come across a guy loving his best friend before?"

"Sure I have." He had, often. And usually the best friend was straight, which made things messy. "But this is different. It's Warren and it's me and he might be moving." The thought made him feel a little gross.

"Mmm. He might. But you need to look at this somewhat rationally, Silas. Aside from this date tonight, which I'm putting firmly in the summer-fling category since no matter what, he's leaving *here* in September, Warren does not date. I suspect that he wouldn't even date you during the school year. Correct?"

"He might." He totally wouldn't, and pretty much said as much more than once. Silas had gotten part of the message, after all, even if he'd missed some of the details.

Tal gave him a raised eyebrow.

Silas sighed and caved. "Okay, no. Shut up."

"The good news is, though, that he won't date anyone." Tal went to the kitchen and opened the fridge. "Supper?"

"Sure. We have lots of time." Silas sat at the table. "So, he's not dating anyone when he's in school, and it sounds like he'll be in school for a while. He'll find someone like Liam, though."

Tal nodded, pulling cold cuts and cheese out and laying it on the counter. "He will. Can you deal with that?"

"I'll have to." Silas shrugged. "I'm going to be far away for at least another year."

"Right." Tal cut bread. "And you'll be sleeping with other guys."

"I will?"

Tal laughed. And laughed again. "Hey, you haven't even mentioned breaking up with Peter yet."

Silas glared at him. Honestly, Peter hadn't even crossed his mind. "Well, I will."

"Why?" Tal turned around and looked at him. "I mean it, why? Warren isn't going to let you get with him for a year at least; you're both going to be with other people until then. You might fall in love between now and then. Probably not with Peter, I grant you, but maybe."

Silas frowned at the table top. "It's not right to stay with him when I know I'd rather be with someone else, obtainable or not. It's not fair to Peter, I mean."

Tal went back to building sandwiches. "Okay, that makes sense. But you can talk to him about it, let it be his choice. If you tell him that you know it's not a forever thing but you'd still like to hang out and be friends, he might be okay with that. And you should talk to Warren, too. Tomorrow."

It was Silas' turn to laugh. "Hell, no."

"Hell, yes." Tal brought him a huge sandwich and sat across from him with his own. "In fact, I insist. I can mediate, if you want. You two absolutely need to clear the air and lay your cards out. I've been watching this go on and on for far too long. It's time you both manned up and dealt with this."

Silas sighed. Tal was too set on things right then to be swayed. The best he could hope for was being too busy the next day, and Warren being too wrapped up in his date to allow the conversation to drift.

Which, he thought, was totally likely. Smiling, hopeful of at least avoiding that conversation if not another one sometime down the road, Silas ate his sandwich and shifted the conversation around to the nine bands they were going to see in only a few short hours.

Due to a series of unexpected life events, including surprise family obligations, work shifts being traded, phone interviews for TA positions, and Tal's car needing to go to the shop for mystery noises, it was the next weekend before Warren got to see Silas and Tal together.

The three of them managed to find each other early in the morning, before anyone's parents could lay claim to their day, and they took off in Tal's newly quiet car, not really planning where to go. They thought maybe a day of state parks would be good, or even just a city park with wide-open spaces. Warren wanted the sun on his face, and Silas would probably need to run around for a while so he didn't explode.

They brought the Frisbees. Warren had often thought they didn't need a puppy, ever, as long as Silas was around.

They got coffee and doughnuts from a drive-through, and then they drove, listening to morning radio and catching up. Warren had the back seat, which he liked; he could look out the window and listen to them banter, sticking his two cents in when he had them, but it was okay to just listen if he was feeling quiet.

They'd both called him the day after his first date with Jordan, and he'd given them as much as he could—yes, dinner had been good, yes they had a lot to talk about, and yes, Jordan was really nice. No, there hadn't been hot monkey sex, and no, he wasn't getting free books on the side. Yes, he'd like to see Jordan again soon.

The concert had apparently gone well, but for some reason Silas had been subdued about it. Warren had put it down to Silas being exhausted from staying up most of the night dancing. Tal had seemed fine.

The car pulled into a parking lot at the city's green space, by the manmade lake. There was hardly anyone around, and they got out of the car to the song of birds instead of small children playing.

"Our pick of the good spots," Tal said, heading to a picnic table in the sun. "Perfect."

Silas and Warren followed, Silas still with a doughnut and Warren still with coffee. It was shaping up to be a warm day.

"We should find a place to swim later," Warren said.

Silas nodded and climbed up on the picnic table to lie down on top of it. Tal and Warren both poked him in the side until he got off again.

"So," Tal said brightly. "Warren, Silas has something to tell you."

Warren looked at Silas, who was staring at Tal with murder in his eyes. Oh, oh.

Tal slid away, down his side of the table, still smiling. "It's okay, go ahead."

"So very not cool, man." Silas sat and glared, then looked at Warren. "I'm sorry. I didn't know our best friend is an idiot."

Warren rolled his eyes. "I think after all these years, we know the score on who's been an idiot most often."

Tal and Silas looked at each other and shrugged.

"Oh, comedy gold!" Warren finished his coffee. "Okay, so what's up? Is this another intervention? I swear I'm not secretly straight."

"No." Silas sighed. "Or at least, not for you. Tal thinks that you deserve to know that, while I fully appreciate that the way you want to live your life doesn't allow for romantic entanglements other than the occasional fuck buddy, and that you won't be dating anyone for at least two or three or nine years, this summer aside, and while all of that makes sense and I don't want to change it for you, or stop you from going out west to be a famous multiple-degree-getting dynamo—"

"Silas." Tal sounded stern. "You're going to choke on your own tangled sentences. Tell him so you two can discuss it and get on with your lives, for God's sake."

Warren stared at them both, not precisely sure what was going on. "Can I say something first?"

"Depends what it is," Silas said quickly. "If it's can we not talk at all, yes. Or even, let's go get drunk. That'll work, too."

Tal snorted.

"Is this about how I love you and you love me and how we'll try to make it work when I'm not living with a textbook?"

Silas gave him a look that was pure belligerence, and Tal managed to look surprised. Warren sighed. "Look. Here's the thing, Silas. I know you love me, and I know you love me in a way that's not like you love Tal. I know you can easily see us together forever. And that scares the crap out of me, honestly, because I *know* you. I've known you since you were five years old. I know every trick, every game, every honest expression you have, and I know how you love."

Warren stood up, his heart racing and his stomach churning. If he'd known that they were going to have this talk on this morning, he wouldn't have had coffee. It had been building for a year, but here it was, and he had to say his own truth. He'd sworn to himself that he would.

"You love with everything you have. You throw yourself at it like you're a weapon and you consume it. And then... it doesn't stand up. You move on, processing lessons and getting on with your life, and you even manage to avoid breaking hearts, most times. But I'm me, and I'm not one of those guys, and I refuse to be. You love me, but I'm *in love* with you, and I have been for a while. If you want to get with me, if you really, really want to be mine and for me to be yours, you're going to have to prove it."

Tal's surprise had given way to an intensity Warren didn't want to go up against. He forced himself to look at

Silas instead, since it was about him, after all.

Silas was pale, looking back. His lips were slightly parted, like he wanted to speak, but wasn't sure where to start.

"I'll be right back," Warren said quietly. "I'm not leaving. I'm just going to the bathroom over there—I feel a little sick, honestly, and you can have some time to think and get yourself together. I know you weren't expecting to hear any of that."

Silas nodded, still wordless, and Warren turned his back and walked as carefully as he could toward the building which housed the restrooms. He wanted to run, but wouldn't let himself. Hell, he wanted to sit down and shake for a while, but that wasn't going to happen, either.

In the cool interior of the building, Warren looked at himself in the mirror and wondered if he really was going to puke. His hands were shaking, and he had to grip the edges of the sink to make them stop.

In a few minutes, though, he splashed water on his face, dried off, and went back out. He couldn't hide all day, and Silas deserved a chance to tell him to go to hell.

Silas and Tal were right where he'd left them, though Tal had turned fully to face Silas and appeared to be talking to him, rather intently. Warren slowed and then stopped, not wanting to interrupt. But then Tal looked up and smiled at him, one hand waving for him to come on, so on he went. It felt like the first time he'd had to take an oral exam, but this time he hadn't studied at all.

He sat down where he had been, across from them both, and looked at Silas. He tried to relax and be still, which was harder than he thought it should be. He had to put his hands in his pockets so they wouldn't start trembling again.

Silas looked back, appearing to be calm. "Okay," Silas said. He nodded. "Okay. I will. I'll prove to you that you're worth more to me than anyone I've dated, loved, or fucked. That's what you need, and that's what I'm willing to do."

Warren blinked, then looked at Tal. Tal just looked back, smiling ever so slightly, so Warren looked at Silas again. "You will?"

"You sound surprised."

"I guess... I guess I kind of expected you to tell me to go to hell." Warren tilted his head to the side and studied Silas' face. "You're going to prove you're in love with me."

"Uh-huh. Step one is breaking up with Peter, and step two is helping you get into that big, fancy school so you can be successful. After that, we'll see."

"Wait." Warren leaned forward. "You're going to leave your boyfriend and help me move away from you?"

"Yes."

Warren leaned back again, his mind buzzing. "Silas. I'm not going to ask you to be a monk until we can live near each other again. Nor am I willing to get busy with you at this stage." He shook his head. "Tal?"

"Yo."

Warren gave him a look and noted that Silas did, too. Tal merely grinned at them both. "You are not a 'yo' kind of guy. Don't do that ever again."

"Whatever. Anyway, what are you asking me for? Permission for you two to keep banging other people while Silas proves he's in love with you? You're both adults. If you're cool with that, it's no skin off my nose. If nothing else, it'll make my life a lot quieter." He paused. "But we won't tell Olivia unless we have to. In fact, the less she knows about this, the better. Now, are you two going to kiss? 'Cause I can look the other way."

"No," Warren said, rolling his eyes.

"No," Silas said at the same time. He didn't roll his

eyes, though. "Not here, not now."

Warren peered at him, but aside from the twinkle in Silas' eyes, there was no hint as to what his plan might be.

"I suppose I should probably cancel my date with Jordan," Warren said, a little regretfully. "Since you're planning to break up with Peter."

"It's up to you," Silas said, apparently meaning it. "Or you can go and talk about books. It doesn't have to be a date if you don't want it to be. But if you do sleep with him, please don't tell me. I'd rather not know."

Warren nodded. He could do that.

"Well." Tal clapped his hands and rubbed his palms together. "Here's to the next year of entertainment."

"That was your outside voice, Tal," Silas said, just before he pushed Tal off the bench.

Some things didn't change, even when the rest of the world had been turned upside down.

Chapter Ten

Catch and Release

Silas had heard Warren say several things during his speech at the park, but one of the things that stood out—after the fact that Warren was in love with him, of course—was that Silas consumed love and moved on, somehow not breaking hearts. He had no idea if that was true or not, or how he did it if it was true. He'd thought about it a lot, and it was making him paranoid.

This was this first time he'd broken up with someone and been aware of every word he spoke. It was also the first time he'd left someone for someone else, even if he'd have to wait a year or even years for the actual reward of it.

Intensely uncomfortable was a good description of his emotional state, and making it even worse was that Peter appeared to be utterly clueless. He was having a lovely time, chattering away, holding Silas' hand and appearing in every way to be completely oblivious to Silas' mood.

"Hey, can we sit and talk for a minute?" Silas tugged him over toward a sidewalk cafe. "On me. Latte?"

"Sure, thanks." Peter beamed at him.

Silas sighed. "I have to tell you something." A prompt

waiter walked up, just as their butts were hitting the chairs. "Two lattes, thank you."

The waiter nodded and left again, and Silas looked at Peter. "I'm not going to be able to see you anymore. I've recently realized I'm in love with someone, and it's not fair to anyone to keep dating you. I'm really sorry; if I'd been clued in earlier, I would never have led you on."

Peter stared at him for a moment, a half smile turning up one corner of his mouth. "Okay. But I never thought you loved me, Silas. Don't carry so much guilt. We had fun, huh? I wasn't looking to get married. So, who's the lucky guy who's won your heart?"

Silas shook his head. He wasn't going to lay that out for the world yet. "No one you know." Liar, liar. "But he's nice. I'm glad you're not mad."

"Of course not." Peter sat back, still smiling. "I don't suppose he does threesomes? I'm going to miss messing around with you. You're... enthusiastic. I always have fun with you. Plus, you taste good."

Silas blinked rapidly. He'd partaken in his share of talk like that, and even out in public at cafes, but he'd never had cause to imagine Warren in such a position.

Peter seemed to sense his advantage. He waited until the coffee arrived and then leaned forward again to whisper in Silas' ear. "Does he like to suck, or is he more the kind to lie back and be done? Think about it, Silas. We could have a lot of fun, and I promise to go home as soon as the mess is cleaned up."

Silas cleared his throat and moved away a little. "You are a very bad man, and I'm going to miss you."

Peter laughed and sipped his coffee. "You know how to reach me if you change your mind."

By the time Silas got home, it was after midnight and Peter had been whispering things at him for more than an hour. Silas locked himself in his room, got undressed for bed, and called Warren's cell phone.

"Silas? It's late, are you okay?"

"No." Silas stretched out on his bed and looked at the dark ceiling, one hand around his cock. "I just broke up with Peter, who took it so well that he suggested a lot of things the three of us could do together, and I'm so hard I ache. Since you're a part of this, I thought you should know."

Warren made an odd sort of choking sound that settled into laughter. "He what?"

"He started with general ideas, and by the time I dropped him off, he'd worked himself up to the point where I was fucking you and you were sucking him off." He stroked, once. "That was after the part where he sucked me while I rimmed you. Honestly, I had no idea his imagination was that good."

Silas thought he heard Warren suck in a breath. "Of course," he went on, "I got a little stuck on the 'you and me' parts. Take him right out of it, and you're left with you and me, and touching and licking and a whole lot of good feelings."

"Silas." Warren sounded a little wary, like he wasn't sure they should be discussing such matters.

"Say my name again." Silas stroked again, his eyes closed.

"Are you... Silas!" That time it sounded like Warren was scandalized.

Grinning, Silas bit his lower lip. "That's it. Nice and loud."

"I'm totally going to kill you."

"No, you won't." Stroke and squeeze. "I'm not going to make you wait for the end. I just wanted you to know—and I wanted to say good night."

"Don't hang up."

Silas sucked in a breath. "No?"

"No." Warren's voice dropped. "Keep talking to me. Tell me... tell me that you've never done this before."

Silas barely paused. "I haven't." It was true. "I've thought about it once or twice, but I never have." He touched himself carefully, not to make it last but to avoid coming when he shouldn't. "Tell me you haven't."

Warren laughed softly. "Of course I haven't. And I'm not going to. At least not this time."

Silas grinned. "Next time? Can I call you up next week and listen to you?"

"No, not next week." Warren was teasing him. His voice was warm, and Silas thanked digital communications for making it sound like Warren was right there. "But sometime. Maybe."

"Oh, good." Silas went back to work, stroking himself the way he liked it best, his fingers giving the right pressure in all the right places. "I look forward to it."

"That's nice." Warren's amusement was back. "Did you spend a lot of the evening hard?"

"Not until he started talking about you. And then it was just stuck in my mind." Silas let his breath catch. "It was hard to get you out of there, once the images were up, you know."

There was a slight pause that Silas used to get closer to orgasm, dragging his palm over the head of his cock.

"Really?" Warren sounded small, and Silas wasn't sure why; a trick of volume, perhaps, rather than confidence.

"Really." Silas' lower back arched. "Shh. It's good. It's all good."

Warren laughed softly. "You're crazy. Don't drop the phone."

Silas would have laughed at the thought if he could have spared the breath or concentration. He was gripping the phone nearly as tightly as his dick. "Oh. Oh, yeah."

Warren grew so quiet Silas had a momentary worry

that he'd hung up, but then his orgasm crashed and splashed over him and all he could do was react.

"Good night, Silas," Warren said gently. "Sleep well." And then he was gone, before Silas could get himself together enough to say anything.

Tal and Olivia sat next to each other on one side of the table, looking across at Silas and Warren. The four of them had arrived at the restaurant from all different directions, Friday evenings generally being a hard time to mesh schedules, and even though they'd only managed to say hellos and glance at the menu, Tal could already tell that something was wrong.

Silas and Warren were totally avoiding looking at each other, and Warren was even leaning slightly away. For guys who loved each other, they were looking more like they wanted to be as far apart as possible. They were speaking, to each other as well as to Tal and Olivia, but they were most definitely uncomfortable. They weren't joking around, and they were even going so far as to be polite to one another.

"Did you two have a fight?" Tal asked after they'd placed their meal orders. He wasn't going to sit all evening and dance around things. It was his role, usually, to help them navigate the waters after they'd had a disagreement. He figured he might as well get on with it.

They both shook their heads, and Warren checked his phone for missed calls or text messages or something. Tal wanted to reach across the table and take it away from him.

"We're fine," Silas said. He gave Tal and Olivia a very earnest look. "No problem."

Olivia studied them for a moment and then turned to

Tal. "Tal, you might want to take a short walk. I need to talk to them for a minute."

Tal gaped at her, and he wasn't the only one—Silas and Warren looked as surprised as he felt. Olivia had never, in the two years or so that they'd been together, asked to do such a thing. He knew that both Silas and Warren liked her and thought she was a good match for him—Warren especially even seemed to consider Olivia a friend—but it had been very rare and always unplanned when they'd spent time with her if he wasn't present. He didn't mind, as such, but being asked to leave the table was pretty incredible.

"Now, don't go giving me that look." She rolled her eyes at them all. "I want to ask them something and offer some advice, and you, my darling, are not ready to hear it. You think you are, but you're not. Trust me."

Tal snorted, and Warren sighed.

"He's not going to leave now," Warren told her.

"You just guaranteed he'll stay," Silas agreed.

Tal nodded. His guys knew him better than she did, apparently. Then he saw the spark in her eye and groaned. "We've just been set up," he told them. "Damn, you're good."

Silas and Warren exchanged a look.

"She's just managed to let all of us know that she's got stuff to say that I need to hear but might not like, and she's made sure I'll sit through it and not just wander off in the middle, suddenly needing to go to the bathroom or something."

"They're not going to like it much, either," Olivia said. She didn't look too happy.

"Great." Warren slumped in his chair. "I can hardly wait."

Olivia sighed and nodded. "It's going to be grand fun for all of us. But it'll help, maybe." She sat up straighter and looked around them. The place was busy, but not packed, and they weren't pressed right up against the next table. Still, she dropped her voice. "You didn't have a fight or a disagreement at all, did you?"

They shook their heads and Tal leaned on the table, trying to see all of them at once. He was curious but probably felt as wary as they did. Olivia knew what was going on, of course, but she'd never before spoken to either of them about their friendship or anything like it, as far as Tal knew. She had been firmly on the outside, his girlfriend, and that was about it.

Her voice still quiet, almost calming, she went on. "But something happened and neither of you are delighted by it." She looked at Warren. "You, especially, look uncomfortable and like you regret something." To Silas she said, "And you're both apologetic and sweet, trying to smooth things over."

They both looked at the table, and Tal felt his eyes widen. He'd only seen them do that once before, when Warren's mom was letting them have it for a water fight they'd had with not only her car windows down but the window to her bedroom open. She'd been plenty upset with them being careless, and they'd done the exact same thing. They were acting embarrassed and even a little ashamed.

"You had sex?" Tal demanded, his voice a squeak. "You—you!"

Olivia closed her eyes and put a hand on his arm. "Please. Sweetie. Let me handle this. Shut up."

Tal snapped his mouth shut. Warren and Silas were both staring at him with huge eyes, Silas shaking his head.

"They didn't," Olivia said firmly. "But something like that happened and it was in the heat of the moment and neither one of them was ready." She pointed at Warren. "You feel like you gave something away that you weren't ready to give. And you, Silas, feel like you were probably pushy, though you don't remember being that way, and you wonder if you've damaged things already."

Neither one of them said anything, but by the shifting around and glances everywhere but at each other, Tal assumed she was right.

"This is fixable," she said reassuringly. She even leaned over and patted Silas' hand. "You weren't a bully. You were irresistible. You may have been a little overwhelming, but you have good intentions and we can salvage it."

Silas nodded at the table, and Tal saw him give Warren a quick, hopeful look.

Tal wondered if he'd ever looked like that and sincerely hoped not.

"Warren, look at me." Olivia was being very earnest. "You didn't do anything wrong, either. You love him, and you're a young man. You want more for yourself and for Silas, yes, but you can still have that. He loves you back—he's not going to run off after someone else now. You only showed him how great it'll be when you're both at the place where you want to be, ready for all of it. If anything, I suspect you've managed to tie him to you even more." Her look grew wicked. "It's an entirely acceptable and effective way to keep a man, by the way. Isn't it, Talbot?"

Tal refused to answer and tried to look indignant. He wanted no part of this. He was busy trying to wrap his brain around Silas and Warren being all sexy together. In theory, he'd been well aware that it was going to happen, but this was no longer theory. They'd done *something*, and it was strange. All of it was strange. Olivia knowing exactly what was going on was also strange.

"You're a very scary lady," he told her.

"But I'm right." She lifted her chin. "You might not

be ready, and they might not be ready, but it's going to happen when the time comes. I just want to make sure everyone gets to the same place at the same time." She smiled suddenly. "I'm a romantic, and this is too good to fall apart." She sat back in her seat and sipped her iced tea, looking impossibly beautiful.

Tal was going to marry her someday, he thought.

Warren gradually relaxed over the course of the evening. The wine with supper probably helped, and the cocktail later on definitely did, but more than that, it was how the others just let him be quiet and think things over without being on his case to snap out of it or to talk things to death. He wasn't up for talking, and he didn't think they really wanted to have a big, huge heart-to-heart, either.

Olivia might, but she wouldn't push for it. Tal definitely did not, but he'd lost the wild look in his eyes and was back to just being Tal. Granted, a Tal who looked captivated by his girlfriend, but Tal nonetheless. And Silas was Silas, more so by the end of the night when he was cracking jokes and being charming.

The four of them were planning how they were going to get their things back to school and into the dorms. Between the four of them, they had the use of three cars, but there were complications. Warren had hoped to just keep his mother's car for a week, and then come back the second weekend for another load and she'd drive him up and take her car away with her, but she was sounding reluctant.

Silas was planning the same thing, and it looked like that would work. Olivia's dad was lending her his pickup, so she was taking all her things at once, and some of Tal's;

Tal was trying very hard to farm out boxes wherever he could to get the rest there.

"You know, we might want to look into renting a van and doing you and me together," Warren said. "It can't be that expensive. It's not like we have furniture. I bet a cargo van or the smallest sized U-Haul would do all of us, even."

"If there's any left." Silas pulled out his phone and sent an e-mail to himself to check it out.

"I'm out," Olivia said with a shake of her head. "Can't afford anything, sorry."

"Let me know." Tal liked the idea. "God, look at the time. I have to work tomorrow."

He and Olivia got up and took their bill. "Call me about that," Tal said, before they said good night and left.

"Are you ready to go?" Warren finished his drink in what was probably too big a gulp, but he wasn't going to waste it.

"Yeah, I guess." Silas shrugged. "Do you have to work or volunteer tomorrow?"

"No. Just help my mom with a few things around the house. She saves up all the jobs for me, and I want to get them done before school goes in—I hate coming home for the weekend and spending it cleaning gutters."

Silas nodded. "Same." He stood up and tugged at his hoodie. "Walk or the bus?" he asked as they made their way to the register to pay.

Warren thought about it. The bus would be faster, assuming they didn't have to wait for it very long, but they probably should talk about things. "Walk. It's a nice night."

Silas nodded and they paid their bills, not saying anything else until they were out and strolling down the block.

It was warm, the late summer holding on as tightly as it could, and there were a fair number of people out, either heading to bars or to places to eat. The atmosphere was almost like a street party, though there weren't enough people out for that. The sensation of everyone trying to get their last blast in was almost palpable, and the two of them turned off the main street quickly, heading down quieter side streets as they made their way to the suburbs.

Warren struggled with how to address what had happened. Olivia had been very close to the truth with her assessment, with only minor qualifications. He had woken up the night after that phone call feeling dismayed and frustrated with himself. He wanted Silas to fully and completely understand before they got to that stage, and Warren hadn't even been able to make him wait a week. He was pathetic.

How could he expect the very highest of effort from Silas when he couldn't even stop himself from being a cocktease?

"I don't think Tal was ready to know that you and me loving each other is eventually going to lead to sex," Silas said mildly, startling Warren out of his thoughts. "He looked like he was going to have a stroke."

Warren shrugged one shoulder and couldn't quite keep a smile from his lips. "Olivia didn't seem to mind the idea."

"That's because Olivia is cool." Silas shoved his hands into his pockets as they walked. "And right. I'm sorry I didn't have better judgment, Warren. I didn't mean to make things weird. I shouldn't have called you like that."

"It's okay," Warren said with a sigh. "I didn't let you hang up. I invited more, and teased you. Olivia was right in that it was the heat of the moment. I feel kind of dumb now. I don't like the idea of leading you on, and I don't want you to be mad that I'm not going to have sex with you for a long time. I'm not even trusting myself with anything more than a handshake now." He rolled his eyes.

"I give good handshakes, so I don't blame you. You could totally lose control." Silas nodded seriously.

Warren bumped their shoulders together, shoving Silas around on the sidewalk. "You know, I adore how modest you are."

"Your sarcasm wounds me to the core." Silas laughed and pushed him back. "We're okay, right? We can mark this up to something that happened once and move on? As much as I'd love to convince you that we can just get down to it and start off being us now, I know that's not what you want, not what you're ready for."

"I'm not," Warren said, keeping his voice as calm and matter-of-fact as he could. "I'm sorry if that hurts you, Silas. I'm not trying to. I'm trying to give us the best chance I can. When it comes to you, the stakes are so high that I just don't want to make a mistake."

Silas gave him a long look that straddled a line between amused and serious. "If anyone but you said that, I'd be laughing my ass off. But I get it. I do. If we do this wrong we can't ever get back to being just best friends, at least not easily and without a lot of distance. I can be patient for you. As long as you know it's going to be difficult."

Warren smiled slightly. "For me, too. And that's kind of the point."

"Uh-huh." Silas nodded and they walked in silence for a couple of blocks. "I'm glad you're here until Christmas, at least, and not leaving in September. I want to keep an eye on you. I want to be able to show you that I'm proving it, too. That'll be easier while we're in the same town."

"I can't wait to see it." Warren reached out and looped his arm through Silas' with a grin. "I have every faith in you."

Silas grinned back. "For Christmas I'm asking for a kiss."

"Hell, you'll get that far before Thanksgiving, I'm sure." Warren rolled his eyes yet again. "I have every faith in you."

Laughing, Silas nodded. "I'll work toward it."

"No more middle of the night calls, though. No phone sex."

"No phone sex." Silas crossed his heart. "No telling you about jerking off."

"Right. Thank you."

"But I'm totally going to do it."

"Me, too."

"Okay." Silas looked at him and smiled. "Trying again. Prove it, take two. We're good?"

"We're good." Warren nodded, pleased. "Oh, and our mothers don't find out for as long as we can keep it from them."

He felt Silas shudder, the tremor rolling right through them both. "Deal."

Chapter Eleven

The Old College Try

Silas bided his time for the first week or two of the fall semester, his attention split between settling into a new semester and pondering what all, exactly, was going to be involved with showing Warren how serious he was about them being a couple. It was a hard balance to get in the first weeks; his time wasn't being eaten by class work or the GSA yet, but Warren was too busy with his extra classes to really sit down and give him a full day of discussion.

"He doesn't want to do that anyway," Olivia told him, after she stopped laughing when he'd said as much. "Have you lost all your good sense? You're love-dumb, my friend. Totally stupid."

"That's not super helpful," he told her, slightly hurt. "This is his gig, after all. I'd be all about just getting together and letting it happen, but he wants it all done right."

She gave him a hard look and he sighed. "Yes, okay. I want it right, too. I'm just not sure what right looks like in this case."

"Well, what does it look like in other cases?" Olivia

looked around Cafe Sol. "Say you were interested in one of those guys over there. How would you let him know?"

Silas held his coffee mug with both hands and tried not to slop any onto his notes from Entrepreneurship Finance. "From a cold start?"

She seemed to consider that. "No, I can figure out the whole introductions and flirting part. Tell me how you take things from that whole liking each other part to seeing each other exclusively part. How does that work?"

"Aside from sex?"

"Yes." Olivia arched an eyebrow at him. "Aside from that. Because we're not doing that with Warren, right?"

"Right." Silas nodded. "Not even a little."

"It's killing you, isn't it?" She laughed at him, teasing. "Poor honey."

"It's not even just the not having sex with Warren part," Silas confided, whispering at her. "It's the no sex at all. I haven't been with anyone in weeks and weeks and weeks. I'm not used to this."

"Lucky for you, it won't kill you. And I happen to know that there's an over-abundance of porn in your dorm. Surely some of it will appeal to you."

Silas sighed. No sympathy at all.

"So?" she prompted. "Before Tal arrives and makes us study. How would you show another guy that you're into him?"

Silas turned to a new page in his notebook. "Well, the obvious stuff first. Dinner out, a movie or two, both at the theater and in my room for privacy. A lot of texting, a lot of time studying together. Outdoor stuff on the weekends, like walking or hiking or going to school events. Dancing."

"Basic dating stuff, huh?"

"Yeah." He looked at the blank page and wrote down 'no dates.' "Things that Warren mostly can't do, since he's trying to graduate early and flat out doesn't want to do, since he doesn't have time. Plus, we already know each other better than anyone else. The need to spend time together getting to know each other just doesn't exist."

She nodded, looking thoughtful. "So it has to be Warren-specific."

"Right. But what?" He drank coffee, annoyed with how difficult this was going to be. He had no doubt at all that Warren was expecting something, maybe even a specific something.

A shadow fell over the table. "Hey, how are you?" Tal leaned forward and kissed Olivia, then went to the counter.

Silas turned in his chair to talk to him while he waited. "Have you talked to Warren today?"

"Yeah, this morning. Saw him at breakfast. He's got class until three, but nothing until after supper, then."

Silas glanced at his watch. Two-fifty. "Cool." He sent a text, telling Warren where they were, and then flipped his notes back to actual work. "If you think of anything, let me know, okay?"

Olivia nodded. "Keep me in the loop if you want. I want to help if I can."

Tal sat. "Help with what?" He handed out another round of coffee and broke a muffin in half to share with Olivia.

"Bringing the two lovebirds together." She smiled at Tal and kissed him again. "You smell nice. Did you come from the gym? You smell like soap."

Tal nodded and ate his half of the muffin. "Four miles on the treadmill. I have a test tomorrow in social psychology, can you believe it?" He pulled out his books.

Silas drank his coffee and worked his way around an idea that was trying to form at the back of his mind.

Warren came back to his room from a meeting with the head of his department, his mind full of options and deadlines. The school in California had been impressed with his proposed line of study but wanted an introductory paper and presentation by the middle of October so they could secure his funding. He knew what he wanted to build around his thesis, but he wasn't sure how, exactly, he was going to find the time to get it all done.

He let himself into his room—shared once more, but with a new roommate. He couldn't get a single room to himself once it was noted on his file that he was slated to graduate after the fall semester. The first thing he noticed when he went in was that the room was trashed, again. The second thing was a note on his neatly made bed, saying that the theater troupe was meeting that night at seven and he should be there.

"Great." Warren sat at his desk and unpacked his bag. If he hurried, he could at least grab some supper before going to the meeting. He'd stay long enough to withdraw his services and then he could get another couple hours of work in before bed.

"Hey, you." Silas looked in the open door and smiled at him. "Busy day?"

"Yeah." Warren sighed. "Come on in. I'm heading to supper in a minute, just need to sort out some stuff."

"I just came from there." Silas came in, bearing a bag of take-out from the Pita Pit. "Thought I might save you some time in a lineup for food."

Warren stared at the bag for a moment, then moved a stack of books to the bed to make room for it on his desk. "Thank you." Between walking to the dining hall and back, waiting in line, and fighting for a table, Silas had just given him half an hour. "I appreciate it."

Silas smiled and put the bag down on the desk, then sat on the bed. He picked up the note as Warren started eating. "Theater meeting, huh?"

Warren nodded. "Can't do it this year. No time."

"That sucks." Silas sounded disappointed. "I know you enjoyed it."

"It was fun, but it was a lot of stress, too." Warren ate. "I can do without the stress, honestly." He told Silas about the meeting he'd just come from and about the work he'd just had added to his plate. "It's all doable, I know. But I'm kind of freaked out about how important this paper feels. Dr. Warner says it's just so they can have something in their files and it's all red tape, but I can't help but think that if it's not up to graduate-level work, they'll change their minds."

"They won't." Silas stood up. "They won't, because you're brilliant and you'll be the star of their whole program. Trust me. You'll do just fine."

Warren smiled at Silas, his stomach feeling full and warm. "Thanks. And thanks for supper. Are you going?"

"To the library for a bit. I have some research to do, and it gets loud in there by eight. I'll come by again before bed, make sure you're not working yourself to death."

Warren laughed. "See you later, then." For a moment he thought maybe Silas was going to kiss him, but he just smiled and left. Warren was pleased.

Tal watched Silas watching Warren study and decided it was time to have a little talk to his best bud. Not so much *with* his best bud, but definitely *to* him.

He kicked Silas under the table. "Hey. Come with me for a minute." He stood up. "Warren. Don't let anyone take our seats, okay?"

Warren didn't look up from the periodical he was reading, but he did wave a hand. Two people down at the other end looked up, though, and Tal smiled at them until they looked back down at their books.

Silas got up, apparently with great reluctance, and left his pen on his stack of loose-leaf notes. He followed Tal out of the study area and into the stacks, then out into the third floor lobby. Thank God, because Tal really didn't want to bodily drag him, and it was rapidly getting to that point.

"What's up?" Silas asked, looking genuinely curious.

Tal reached out and gave the back of Silas' head a gentle slap. "You, my smitten kitten, need to get a freaking grip, do you hear me?"

Silas opened his mouth, but Tal kept right on going.

"You will not sit there and stare at him. You will not write little love notes. You will not send him flowers and you will not write him poetry. You will grow a pair and get yourself back into a proper state of mind to be serious about school and your own life or you will not graduate at all, never mind on time, while he's leaving early. You will do everything you can to have a full and complete life as Silas Cook, and you will stop acting like a fourteen-year-old girl. Got it?"

Then he turned on his heel and marched back to the table to work on his communications homework. Honestly, some days it was just too much.

Ten minutes later, Silas hadn't come back, so Tal sent him a text message asking where he was.

"Dissing you to your girlfriend."

Warren was still working away, typing on his computer, looking up more data, then typing again.

Tal sighed. "Warren."

"Mmm. Just a sec."

"Warren."

Warren looked up, blinked slowly a couple of times, and rejoined the physical world. "Oh, hey. Where's

Silas?"

"I bitched him out and now he's slagging me off to Olivia."

Warren nodded. "Good for him. What did you bitch at him for?"

"Staring at you instead of studying."

Warren blinked again, then slowly smiled. "Yeah? Well, good for you. He should be studying, not staring."

"That's what I said. But I meant it."

Warren smiled more and went back to typing at his computer, this time with more vigor.

Tal sighed. "I just don't get it, I guess."

At Thanksgiving they all went home, and Tal went to Olivia's for the weekend, much to his parents' delight. Tal told Warren and Silas that they were assuming he was going there so he could propose to Olivia.

"You're only twenty-one years old," Silas said, his eyes horrified.

"I know. She'd say no anyway. She has a plan, you know? We'll get married after she's finished her pharmacy degree and we've both been working for a while. Of course, we're going to live together first, I think. But married? Now?" He shook his head.

"Are they going to be mad that you weren't home for Thanksgiving and then came back without a promise of a wedding?"

Tal shrugged. "I think I'll be close to home for Christmas."

Warren and Silas both had family commitments with their mothers and extended families, but they managed to find time to escape the madness on Friday. They skipped the shopping and had a very late lunch instead, then went to a movie. Warren smiled when Silas bought a large popcorn for them to share, and had to stifle a laugh when they brushed fingers in the tub.

Silas winked at him.

By the end of the movie, they'd turned it into a game and tangled their fingers five times, and Warren was convinced that Silas was the best-smelling person on the planet. He was trying to figure out what scent Silas was wearing when he realized that every single time he'd seen Silas since school had gone back in, Silas had showered and changed clothes within no more than an hour or so. He was always, without fail, neat and clean and fresh when they saw each other.

The credits rolled on the movie, and Warren stayed sitting until they were done, making the other people in their row go out the other side. Silas snickered but didn't say anything. Finally, the theater empty and the house lights up, Warren turned to look at him.

"Happy Thanksgiving. I'm thankful for you."

Silas blushed. "I'm thankful for you, too."

"Would you like to kiss me?"

"Here? Now?" Silas looked around. "For real?"

Warren nodded. "Yeah. For real. Here and now. Kiss me, Silas."

Silas stared at him, a half-smile on his face. Then he touched Warren's cheek with the backs of his fingers and leaned forward to kiss him gently. It wasn't a peck, and it wasn't a full-on assault, but it was a very serious kind of kiss, a kiss that lingered and meant all kinds of things. It was the kiss of a promise.

Warren accepted it, smiled, and gave him one more back. They were well on their way.

Chapter Twelve

Fumbling Toward Ecstasy, Take Two

D on't look like that," Warren hissed. They were back at school, and Silas was still giving him pleased little smiles and smug winks. "Olivia is going to think I put out, and then she'll give me a huge lecture." He crossed the dorm lobby to the wall of mailboxes and unlocked the one for his room. Four envelopes, a dorm notice, and a magazine about motorcycles. That was for his roommate.

Silas laughed, apparently unconcerned if Warren got a lecture or not. "She won't. Tal tells her everything, and I told Tal that nothing happened other than some hand-holding at the movies and one kiss. Completely true." He checked his mail as well and came away with the dorm notice.

"I suppose. Are you going to the dining hall for supper?" Warren walked to the stairwell, flipping through his envelopes. Two for him, one of them yet another pre-approved credit card he didn't want. The other though, was from the graduate school of the Department of Sociology, Stanford University. He held it up to show Silas.

"What does it say?" Silas stopped walking, and they stood in the hallway blocking traffic while Warren shoved the other mail under his arm and opened the letter. "Did they get your funding?"

Warren scanned the letter quickly and nodded. "Got my funding in place, made sure my name is on the list for graduate housing, and look forward to meeting me in January." He looked up from the letter, a little off balance. "I'm going to grad school. In two months."

Silas gave him what could only be called a brave smile and nodded. "You're amazing. Congratulations, Warren." Then Silas hugged him, right there by the stairs, and didn't let go.

Warren relaxed into him and held him back, his letter in one hand, arm wrapped around Silas' shoulders. "Thanks. I'm a little stunned, actually. And kind of scared."

"You'll do great." Silas spoke softly. "You're made for this. They came looking for you, right? You're going to impress the hell out of them."

"Will you come visit?"

Someone came down the stairs and said something as he pushed past, but Warren didn't care what.

"Of course." Silas hugged him harder and then let him go. "Yes. Spring break.""

Warren nodded and they started up the stairs. "I'd like that. How are you going to manage it?"

"I've been saving for plane tickets ever since you mentioned this in the summer. I've got enough to come to you twice before next fall."

"Seriously?" Warren slowed his steps and looked at Silas, searching his face. "For real?"

"Yep." Silas gave him a sunny grin. "I'm looking into the cost of living and stuff, too. I'm not sure if I'm ready to leap into business yet, but I'm sure I can figure out some viable way to move there while you're going to school. If nothing else, I've applied to their business school for a certificate in entrepreneurship. It's hard to get in, though, so don't count on it."

Warren stopped entirely. "You're picking schools so you can be with me?"

"Well, yes." Silas tilted his head at Warren. "Of course I am. It helps that it's a great school, but I probably would have applied wherever you went. You didn't know that?"

Warren looked at the door in front of them. Silas' floor. He opened the door and started down the hall to Silas' room, stuffing the mail into his backpack as he went. Silas came right along behind him, not saying anything but getting his key out.

They went into Silas' room—tiny, mostly tidy, a single for a senior student—and Warren dropped his backpack on the floor.

Silas looked at him warily. "What?"

"You're going to follow me."

"Yes." Silas nodded and put his own backpack on the chair. "I intend to, anyway. We'll see if it works out."

Warren reached for him, one hand tugging on a shirtsleeve to pull him close and the other sliding along Silas' jaw. "I love you."

Silas smiled at him and then kissed him, not hesitating at all. Warren met him with tongue and teeth, the grip he had on Silas' shirt letting go so he could hold him better and keep him right there, as close as he could be. They didn't move from standing, but they kissed each other, tasting and testing and exploring until they had to pull back to breathe.

"You didn't realize I was going to come to you?"

"I'm not sure I really thought about it," Warren admitted. He didn't let Silas go. "I just had this vision of work and more work and being online with you a lot.

And with Tal, but that didn't seem so vital."

Silas smiled again. "I like being vital. Wanna make out for a bit?"

"Yes. But I need to call my mother. Can I come back this evening after supper?"

Silas nodded. "By which you mean after supper and homework."

Warren blushed. "I'll bring it with me. We'll test ourselves."

"Okay." Silas was grinning at him. "Kiss me again and get out of here before I try to trap you."

Warren kissed him again, this time slowly and deeply, taking his time and making it as good as he possibly could. He let Silas go only after he'd gotten a moan and knew that he'd made his point. "I'll see you later, at supper?"

Silas nodded and licked his lips. "Don't let Olivia see you."

"I'm not sure I care right now. She can lecture all she wants." He picked up his bag and opened the door, feeling like he should whistle. "Call me when you're leaving for supper."

"Will do."

Warren headed down the hall back to the staircase, smiling so hard his cheeks hurt.

Silas loved him. For real and for sure.

Tal and Silas were already sitting and eating when Warren got there.

"So, I hear you got good mail today." Tal was grinning at him. "Well done, man. Your mom must have ruptured something."

Warren rolled his eyes. "She didn't cry. I think she was saving it up for when we got off the phone." He looked around. "Where's Olivia?"

"Study group." Tal patted the book next to his tray. "And I have one in twenty minutes. Is it just me, or are there more papers and tests this semester than any other so far?"

Warren just looked at him, one eyebrow up. He'd had two extra classes and that awful paper and presentation to do, plus he'd spent the summer doing intersession online.

"Right, wrong person to ask. Never mind." Tal laughed, though, and ate his supper. "Just a couple more weeks. I'm going to sleep the first four days I'm home over break, I swear to God. Nothing but eat and sleep. Maybe video games."

"That sounds great." Silas nodded at him. "And just for a break? A nap."

Warren thought it sounded good, too, but he was reasonably sure that his break would be spent packing, mailing, and trying to find the books he'd need for his first quarter. If he was honest with himself, he could admit he'd probably be getting a head start on his reading, too.

"Know what we're going to do?" Tal asked. A note in his voice made Warren look up at him. "We're also going to make sure Warren doesn't bog down. We're going to have fun and relax."

Warren smiled. They always knew. "You're not going to let me mope at all, are you?"

"Nope." Tal pointed with his fork. "You, young man, are going to arrive at grad school fresh-faced and well rested. Even if it kills me making it happen."

"Aw." Warren laughed and ate his chicken pie. Maybe he'd only start *some* of his reading. Some video games would be fun. First, though, he had four papers to write and six finals to take.

Tal hurried through his meal and rushed off to his study group, promising to have coffee with them the next afternoon, even if they all had books with them, and Silas waited for Warren to finish.

"How much work do you have tonight?" Silas asked as they took their trays to the rack.

"Couple hours, maybe? I have one paper almost done, so I might just take care of that and call it a night in terms of homework. Want to watch some TV if we're both done by nine or so?"

Silas nodded. "Yeah. If by 'watching TV' you mean what we discussed earlier."

"Totally." Warren grinned. "Just a little TV, though. Not a movie."

Silas burst out laughing. "Got it. Come up to my room, the door'll be open. I've got a paper, too, and some stats to work on. Come rescue me by nine."

They walked back to their dorm, and Warren hoped he'd be able to concentrate long enough both to finish his paper and not just barrel into Silas' room at nine. He'd known it was a mistake to become physical while they were both in school, but he had no way to stop it, and no actual desire to put the brakes on any more than he already had. He consoled himself by knowing that all over campus, the majority of the students were probably sexually active, and the majority of the students were not flunking out. Therefore, he and Silas stood a reasonable chance of graduating well.

"You're thinking too much."

"I know, I'm trying to stop," Warren admitted.

"I swear I won't eat up all your time, and I promise you will be as focused as ever. I also promise not to push for a movie."

Warren quirked a smile at him. "For how long? I don't want to tease. I don't want to be mean."

Silas shrugged. "Until after exams, for sure. Winter break might be touchier. You'll be leaving, and that makes it different."

"Okay." Warren nodded as they went into the dorm. "I can understand that."

Silas gave him a discreet pat on the bum. "See you around nine."

Warren tried not to blush.

"My paper probably sucks," Warren said as he walked into Silas' room. "Just so you know. I blame you."

Silas looked up from his laptop and grinned. "Since I know you're totally incapable of a bad paper, I'll accept the compliment. Give me two minutes to finish this spreadsheet. There's soda in the fridge, if you want."

Warren closed the door behind him and made sure it was locked, then went to the fridge. He got a can of soda and sat on the edge of Silas' bed. His hair was still a little damp from the shower, and he noticed with a smile that Silas' was, too. "Are we going to actually watch some television?" he asked, more to tease than anything else.

"Sure. I have a bunch on my external drive. New cop stuff, so you'll hate it." Silas grinned at him and saved his file, then started closing programs. He plugged in his drive, though, and looked through folders. "How about a documentary? It'll be like a test, to see if I can hold your interest."

Warren smiled at him and put the soda can on the desk. "I don't think you need to worry."

"I think you're very sweet." Silas started a TV show and stood up, arranging the laptop so they could see the screen.

"I think you're stalling." Warren's eyes widened. He hadn't meant to say that.

Silas, thankfully, laughed. "Oh, really?" He came close, pushed Warren over to lie on the bed, and straddled his thighs. "You do?"

"You're still talking and not kissing," Warren pointed out. "Although you are touching, and that's good."

"You want good?" Silas leaned forward, his weight on his hands and knees, no other part of him touching Warren. Then he kissed Warren as carefully and with as much intention as Warren had shown him earlier.

"I think," Warren said when he could breathe again, "that we should save those for very special occasions."

Silas smirked. "Oh, I don't know. I wouldn't want you to forget me when you're out west."

Warren looked up at him. "I'm not going to forget you. You've been a part of me my whole life. How many people can say that?"

Silas kissed him again, and this time Warren pulled him down and turned so they were lying on the bed and facing each other. In the background, he could hear the television show, but he didn't care at all what it was. It was just noise.

"I'm going to miss you," Silas whispered between kisses. His hand was resting on Warren's hip, not pushing or pulling.

"I know. I'll miss you, too," Warren whispered back. He kissed Silas' mouth and then his jaw, working his way to the pulse point in Silas' neck. Silas' heart was racing, the blood making flutters under Warren's tongue. He tasted like clean skin and smelled ever so slightly of soap, his shampoo scent stronger. Warren made a soft sound and sucked lightly at the spot.

Silas' fingers tightened on Warren's hip and his head fell back. Warren did it again, careful not to make a mark as he dragged his teeth over the skin. He wanted to lick and suck, but he held back; too much at once would be like overdosing on dessert before enjoying the meal.

When he made his way to Silas' collar, Warren found

himself stopped by not only a T-shirt, but a nicely buttoned overshirt as well. Oh, well. This was, after all, television and not a movie. He made his way back up to Silas' mouth and plunged his tongue in, swallowing a moan.

The hand on Warren's hip slid around to his waist and under his shirt to lie flat on the small of Warren's back. Silas shifted closer and they were pressed tightly together, chest to chest. Warren moved a leg and then they were perfectly lined up, comfortable and easy. Just like that.

Warren wondered just how long it would be possible to lie there, kissing Silas and holding him, without wanting more. He was quickly losing faith in his ability to control himself; he should have realized that back in the summer, the night Silas called him at midnight to jerk off on the phone.

Gasping as Silas' hips shifted and the memory awoke, Warren stilled for a moment and just let himself breathe.

"Are you okay?" Silas whispered, not moving again.

"Yes. Just... testing myself, I guess. Don't rub on me for a bit or I'll come in my pants."

Silas laughed softly. "I know the feeling. Kiss me again."

Warren kissed him, and they filled half an hour with just that, pausing more than a few times to wait out a particularly wonderful rush of endorphins or desperation.

"This is going to keep me up half the night," Silas said, the hand on Warren's back now petting. His lips were red and bruised-looking, swollen from kisses.

"Not me." Warren closed his eyes as Silas' hand pushed down over Warren's ass to stay there. "I'm going to sleep like a baby, right after I jerk off a time or three."

"Naughty." Silas gave Warren's ass a squeeze, and Warren's hips rocked with it. They both froze, not even breathing.

"I should go." He couldn't even move, let alone stand up and walk anywhere. "Silas."

"Shh. God." Silas' voice sounded strained, rough. "Don't say my name like that."

Warren tried. He really, really did. He thought about gross things and ice cubes and his mother. It didn't help. He opened his eyes and Silas was right there, looking back, perfectly debauched and sexy and beautiful, and he could feel the hard line of Silas' erection against his own, both of them so stiff that even rolling apart would hurt. "*Silas.*"

Silas closed his eyes and shook.

"Not your fault," Warren whispered. "I'm not mad."

Silas rolled on top of him and they ground together, Warren's hands tight on Silas' hips, guiding him. Once, twice, and on the third driving thrust Warren came, his back arched and his head tipped back, saying Silas' name again.

He could feel Silas' cock throb through four layers of cloth, but he didn't hear the words Silas was whispering.

Warren knew what they meant, though, and he loved Silas all the more for it.

Chapter Thirteen

New Year, New Start

Tal had been correct—when he came home at Thanksgiving without having given Olivia a diamond ring, his parents had claimed his presence for the entirety of the winter break. Lucky for Tal, Olivia's parents were willing to share, and she was with him for the first two weeks, right up until Christmas Eve.

This meant, of course, that most afternoons found Tal, Olivia, Silas, and even Warren sprawled all over the living room at Tal's house, taking turns with video games and movies. Silas was intent on not letting Warren spend the entire break working on school things before he'd even met his professors face to face. He could do that in the mornings, and then Silas would grab him at noon and not return him to his mother's house until after ten at night.

Silas' mother was getting used to having them tramp in at supper time. "It's like old times," she said. "And I love it. You have no idea how quiet it is here when you're all away at school."

"My mom says the same thing," Warren told her. "She's started up a few dinner clubs, I think."

"We have book club on Tuesday evenings together."

Silas' mother smiled at him. "We spend a lot of time talking about you two, though."

Silas snorted. "How boring."

"No, not since you came to your senses. We're entertaining everyone these days, wondering when you're going to tell us."

Warren almost dropped his fork.

"In three years," Silas said calmly. "Until then, you know nothing. Got it?"

"Yes." She nodded. "I figured it was something like that. Do you have plans you're not telling me?"

Warren looked back and forth between the two of them, not sure if he was supposed to say anything or not.

"Not really. Oh, I'm going to visit him on my spring break. I'll fill you in on the rest as I get the fall sorted out. Not yet."

"All right." She looked at Warren. "You have to promise me you'll work hard and take very good care of yourself out there. We all need you to be healthy and in one piece when he gets to you, or we'll never hear the end of it. He whines."

"I do not!"

Warren chewed and thought about that. "He doesn't really—or at least, not to me. He's patient and hardworking and he lets me study even when he'd rather watch TV." The sudden silence made him look up. Silas was pink and his mother was looking like she'd just been given a gift. "I mean. Um. He whines. Yes."

Silas leaned over and kissed him on the cheek, and then Warren blushed.

Warren opened the door and let Silas in out of the dark and cold. "Did you and Mom pass in the driveway?" he asked, handing Silas a hanger for his coat.

"No, at the corner. We waved. How long is she out for?" Silas handed him the shopping bag with the chips and went to put the beer in the fridge. The movies were already in the living room.

"Most of the night. She said she'd call if she had too much wine; she might stay over." His aunt and uncle had wanted Warren to go over there, too, but Warren suspected his mother had begged off for him, using words like "moving," "boyfriend," and "three more weeks." Suddenly he hadn't been included in the invitation. He would see them all on Christmas Day, anyway.

After that, he'd have a couple of weeks to finish shipping things before he'd be on his way, a week before classes started. He figured he'd need the time to get himself settled in and wander around campus to locate all the important things, like food, coffee, and the best places for take-out. He'd gotten the address for where he'd be living, but until he saw it, he wouldn't be able to tell what he'd need to buy in terms of bookcases and things like that. He'd gotten e-mails from various people in the department and had tentative meetings set up already with teaching assistants and his assigned advisor, but all that Warren could think of was that he wouldn't be with his friends for the first time in his life.

When Silas turned around from the fridge, Warren was right there, reaching for him and hanging on tight. "Oh, hey." Silas held him back, probably startled out of his mind. "It's okay. What's got you so freaked? It's okay." He rubbed a hand down Warren's back and kept hugging him.

"I don't want to go."

"Yes, you do." Silas sounded calm. "You really do. You just want me and Tal to go with you. And Olivia. Right?"

Warren buried his face in Silas' neck. He smelled wonderful. "I want you to go with me. I don't want to leave you."

"That I understand." Silas kept petting him, right there in the kitchen. "And I'll get there as soon as I can, I promise. But you can do this. I know you can. You might have growing pains, but it's all going to be fantastic. I know it will."

Warren sighed and nodded. "Call me all the time, okay? I'll answer, even in class and meetings. I swear I will. And I'll say I love you so everyone who's around can hear, and they'll all know it's hard for me to be there, but that someone, somewhere loves me and is cheering me on."

Silas laughed softly. "All right. I will, mostly because it'll take me forever to know when you're in class and it'll be by accident. But they're going to cheer you on, too, and they'll love you. Not the same as me, but they will."

Warren thought maybe Silas was a little optimistic about that stuff, but he let it pass.

"Better? Want a beer now?" Silas let him go. "A little beer, we'll watch some TV or a movie, and we'll just start making out when your mother will come home."

"Or call and say she's not coming home. I have my fingers crossed."

Silas gave him a long look and got two bottles from the fridge. They'd only just gone in, but they were chilled; he might have had them in the cooler at his place. "Has she ever done that?"

"Well, no." Warren shrugged. "She could, though."

Silas took his hand and they went to the living room. "Let's watch some TV and relax a bit. I think that black and white thing is on tonight—*A Christmas Carol*."

Warren nodded. Apparently he was feeling a little emotional. "Sorry. I didn't intend to get all clingy like that."

"I like the cling." Silas wiggled his eyebrows and passed Warren the remote. "I like the cling a lot. But if we're going to watch some TV with our TV—if you get my meaning—I'd like you to be a little more balanced. Feel free to cling, though."

Warren took his meaning and found the right channel on the television before curling up with him on the couch, their legs tangled together. "Merry Christmas," he said, toasting Silas with his beer bottle.

"And to you." Silas raised his bottle and they both drank. "The best one yet."

Warren smiled at him, and they watched the end of some Christmas cartoon, waiting for their show to start. It was all going to be okay. It really was, even if he was going to be sad for the first couple of days. He was going to a great school, the department was excited about his work, and Silas was going to come see him in March. He wasn't going to have a roommate, with any luck, and it was all going to be okay.

Warren drank his beer and petted Silas' leg, taking comfort in being home and the complete normalcy that surrounded him. Things were going to get weird soon; he'd better soak it up while he could.

"You're thinking again."

"I guess." He sighed and finished his beer, then leaned forward to put the bottle on the table. "Distract me."

Silas shifted to put his own empty bottle down. "Come here. I love it when you invite this, by the way. Take off your shirt."

Warren lifted his eyebrows as Silas got up, taking the blanket off the back of the couch and putting it on the floor.

"Massage. Cheap-ass and probably not very good, but get on the floor and let me rub your back. You're so tense I can feel it when I'm not even touching you. Do you have any oil or cream or anything?"

"My room. Oh, wait, there's some oil in the bathroom—it's not scented or anything, my mom just uses it in the bath for her dry skin. It's under the sink." Warren peeled off his shirts and took off his belt. "It's not approved for use with condoms. Just sayin'."

Silas snorted and headed to the bathroom.

Warren thought a moment. "The stuff in my room is, though."

He thought he heard Silas miss a step and smiled. He loved that he could do that, and would miss it when it was gone. He got another couple of bottles from the fridge and took them to the living room, meeting Silas on the way. "When you're ready."

"After I rub your back, probably." Silas gestured to the floor and rolled up his sleeves.

Warren stretched out on his stomach. "Oh, it's starting." On the TV, the black and white movie was beginning, introducing Ebenezer Scrooge to them. Warren made sure he could see from where he was, but as soon as Silas straddled his thighs and the lid of the oil snapped, he closed his eyes. It was like a reflex; back rubs meant closed eyes.

He heard Silas rubbing his palms together and then Silas' hands were on him, starting at his shoulders, coasting on a thin film of oil. He had warm hands, and while the massage was far from trained, it was probably exactly what Warren needed. All through the first portion of the movie, right through the first commercial break, Silas rubbed and kneaded and pressed away knots until Warren's back felt warm and glowing. His shoulders weren't tense, his lower back didn't ache, and his spine felt like it was an inch longer.

"Okay?" Silas brushed over his skin with one hand, no longer rubbing, just touching.

"Uh-huh. Thank you." Warren opened his eyes. "I think the beer got warm."

"I'll trade them for cold ones. They're not open yet." He got up off of Warren and went to the kitchen. Warren rolled over, looking for his shirts.

He tugged the T-shirt back on, but left the overshirt off, then sat on the couch again just as Silas came back with cold bottles. "Thanks," he said again.

Silas sat down and kissed him, passing a bottle. "My pleasure."

Warren reached for the remote and muted the TV. "Do you want to know how you proved it to me?"

Silas leaned back and looked at him. "I kind of assumed it had something to do with not dating anyone else."

"Partly." Warren nodded. "I knew that you either weren't sleeping with anyone, or if you were, that you were being very discreet, both of which I appreciated. But mostly it was stuff like this. You had me half naked on the floor and we're alone—you didn't push. You always, for months now, made sure that you were clean and fresh when you knew you'd see me. You brought me food to give me what I needed, which was time. You never complained. You never pushed. You waited for me to go at my pace. Silas, you're the most enthusiastic go-get-'em person I've ever known. Your entire life, you've just had things happen for you, immediately and easily." Warren took Silas' hand. "But because I said wait and go slow, you did. I told you to prove it to me, and you did. You gave me every single thing I said I needed, and then you topped out by making an effort to come to where I'll be. Even if you don't go to school there and can't live near me for a while? You proved it. I know you love me, without any doubt at all."

By the time Warren stopped talking, tears were pricking

at his eyes again, and Silas was red in the face and biting his lower lip. "How am I supposed to respond to *that*?" he said, laughing nervously. "I do love you, Warren. All of me is for all of you."

Warren smiled and stood up. "Bring your beer." He let go of Silas only to grab his cell phone so he could text his mom to stay the night, thanks. Then he put the phone on the coffee table and took Silas' hand again. "Come on."

Silas took his beer and had a large swallow before going with Warren, down the hallway to his room. "Are you—"

"Yes. I'm sure." Warren nodded and Silas smiled at him, lifting his bottle in another toast. Warren laughed, clinked their bottles together, and drank. "Can we please get to the bedroom?"

The cell phone chirped.

Silas laughed ruefully. "Don't look now, but your seduction scene is falling apart. I think we might just have to screw around instead."

"This is what happens when I don't have a plan." Warren pointed to his room. "You go in there. Put on some music or the TV or something, if you want. I'll be right there."

Silas kissed the tip of Warren's nose and went. "I'm turning off my phone, by the way."

Warren nodded and went to get his. "Me, too, as soon as my mother says she's not coming home." He looked at the screen, snorted at the admonition to play safe and have breakfast ready when she got home, and turned it off. There, everything was fine and ready.

It was time to release a little pent-up tension. Finally.

Warren went down the hall, leaving the TV on and the lights shining. They'd be back up, he was sure, even if it was only for more beer and the bag of chips. "Do you know," he asked as he walked into the bedroom, "how long I've been wanting to do this?"

"A year? A bit more?" Silas was at the stereo on the other side of the room, amidst the half packed boxes.

"Longer. Years. No pressure." Warren grinned at the look Silas gave him and tugged his T-shirt off. "Come here." He moved to the bed and pulled the covers down.

Silas turned the music on and walked to the bed from his side, unbuttoning his shirt. "I assume your mother took your kind invitation to stay away?"

"And she told me to play safe. I'm trying not to think about it." He did, however, open the drawer of his nightstand and take out the lube and rubbers. "Honestly, I have no idea what she thinks we're going to get up to." He undid his jeans and shoved them off, along with his socks, then got on the bed wearing only his briefs.

"She has an over-active imagination," Silas agreed. He undressed as well and joined Warren, reaching for him and pulling him down for a kiss.

"We need to stop talking about her now." Warren looked down at Silas' face and nodded. "Deal?"

"Deal." Silas' hand trailed up the inside of Warren's thigh. "Can I suck you?"

Warren got a little dizzy as his blood all flowed downward. "Um, yes. Yes."

Silas laughed softly and kissed him, his hand almost tickling. "Easy there. No passing out." His knuckles brushed Warren's balls.

"I'm nowhere near passing out." Warren kissed him back and mapped out Silas' chest with his hands. "You feel amazing."

"And we're not even to the fun part yet."

"Yeah, we are." Warren nuzzled Silas' cheek. "We're together. It's the fun part."

Silas turned his head and kissed him, and they shifted and rolled on the bed, just touching and moving together for a few minutes. Warren could feel his heart rate picking up, his breathing becoming shallow, and he pushed Silas away for moment. "You make me lose control," he said, dipping his head to mouth at Silas' chest.

Silas nodded, one hand in Warren's hair. "Same. God. Do that again."

Warren licked at one nipple, then bit it lightly. He dropped a hand to palm Silas' cock over his boxer briefs. Silas was hard, his prick long and thick. Warren rubbed at it through the cloth and teased the nipple until Silas arched up into his hand. Then he tugged the waistband of Silas' underwear down and held Silas' cock for the first time.

Silas hissed, his hips going still. "Don't get fancy."

"Just looking." Warren kissed Silas chest and sat up, his fingers curling around what he wanted to see. He moved down the bed and licked, unable to resist.

"God, Warren." Silas fell back on the bed. "I'm supposed to be doing that to you."

"You will." Warren was sure. He licked again and tugged Silas' underwear off. "Jesus, you're beautiful." He cupped Silas' balls and rolled them in his palm.

Silas made a noise and his legs slid on the sheets. "Warren."

Warren bent over him and licked again, pressing his tongue into the root of the shaft and then wetting Silas' sac. He could feel Silas losing his calm, could feel him starting to come apart under Warren's mouth, but that was good. He licked and sucked and lifted his head only far enough to take Silas' erection into his mouth. Silas made a broken sound, his hands fisting in the sheet and then in Warren's hair. As soon as Silas' fingers tangled in his hair, Warren stopped moving—and he used his hands to encourage Silas' hips to thrust.

"Warren!" Silas shattered, thrusting and rocking into

his mouth and throat, fucking Warren's face with long strokes that became uneven quickly. When Warren felt Silas get even harder, he pulled off, wet a finger, and pressed it at Silas' hole.

Jets of come shot up Silas' abdomen, his whole body curling with the shock and release of his climax. Warren laid his head on Silas' thigh and soothed him through it, petting and kissing lightly until Silas' hand once more brushed his hair. "Come here," Silas whispered. "Come up here with me."

Warren moved up, lying down with him and taking long, slow kisses as Silas curled into him. The touches and pets were deliberate and sweet as Silas caressed his back and chest and arms. He wasn't bringing Warren down, and he wasn't working himself up; he was just taking his time and tasting what he could, as far as Warren could tell. Warren didn't care. They had all night and a few days and then the rest of their lives.

"Take these off." Silas nudged him, then knelt up to help Warren shed his briefs—with a grin, Silas wiped off his stomach with them, making Warren laugh. "Now. Let's see." He pushed Warren down onto his back and followed Warren's example by exploring quite intensely. He didn't lick, though, apparently aware that all that would achieve was a fast orgasm and then cuddling for a while. "Pass me one of those rubbers," he said, holding a hand out. His other hand was firmly wrapped around Warren's dick.

Warren did as he was bid, not bothering to ask any questions. Wherever they were going, it was going to be wonderful, and they were getting there together. He watched as Silas rolled the rubber down onto Warren's erection and wiggled happily as Silas stroked him.

"Lube?" Silas looked at the table and held his hand out again.

Warren took it and put some on Silas fingers, then a bit more when Silas asked for it. "What's the plan?" he asked as he put it back, out of the squish zone.

"Give me your hand." Silas crawled over Warren's legs. When Warren offered his hand, Silas smeared it with lube and caught him at the wrist. "Now..." He moved up, straddling Warren's hips, and pulled Warren's hand back and down.

Warren's eyes went wide as he caught on. He didn't ask if Silas was sure—he clearly was. So Warren did what he wanted to do—what Silas wanted him to do—and slid slippery fingers over soft skin and pressed in. He watched Silas' face, taking in every flutter of his eyelashes, every sigh, every twitch of a smile and sign of a moan before he could hear it. When Silas' body opened to him, his face relaxed and he smiled, looked down at Warren. "Love you."

"Love you, too." Warren swallowed hard. "Ready?"

"I've been ready for ages." The hand on Warren's cock gave a squeeze and Silas moved back and down, waiting only long enough for Silas to help him get in the right position, and then he was sinking down.

"Dear God." Warren closed his eyes. "Silas?"

"Now is not the time to say my name." Silas shifted a little. "Oh, yeah. Maybe it is."

Warren laughed and Silas swore. Eyes open because he couldn't not see this, Warren looked up at Silas and smiled. "On three."

"On three what?" Silas *squeezed*, grinning.

"God damn it." Warren braced his feet and rocked his hips, back and forth.

"*Oh*!" Silas' eyes went wide and his grin faltered. "Oh, God. Do that again."

Warren did, his hands on Silas' hips, guiding him. "Can I say your name?"

"Yes. Yes, say it." He lifted a little and fell back, finding Warren's rhythm. "Say anything you want."

Warren thrust into him again and again, his legs helping to lift his hips faster as Silas sped up. When Silas braced one arm on the bed and took his dick in hand to jerk off, Warren broke. "Silas!" His back arched and he fucked wildly, with no control at all other than to keep himself inside this perfect place, this beautiful shining moment with Silas. He could feel the moment growing, sparkling and glittering like snow or sand, and finally Warren had to close his eyes against the inevitable.

"Silas." With a whisper of a prayer, Warren came while Silas lay on top of him, his own orgasm draining him of strength.

With only a couple of weeks to go, they'd found perfect, and Warren would take that with him to keep him going until Silas could reach him.

Epilogue

W arren stood by the baggage claim and tried not to bounce, push anyone out of the way, or in any way get himself ejected from the airport. The flight was there, on the ground, and he even had a car so they didn't have to wait for a taxi. Of course, renting a car for the week cost more than a taxi would have, but if Silas could save for the plane ticket, Warren could rent a car so they could have the freedom to do what they wanted.

People started coming toward the luggage carousel for Silas' flight, and the lady closest to Warren started waving. That was a good sign, Warren assumed, and he looked hard, searching for Silas' face. A man bent down to scoop up his kid, and there Silas was, looking tired but perfectly *there*.

Warren didn't hesitate, just walked right to him and kissed Silas full on the mouth. "I've missed you so much."

Silas looked startled, then delighted. "I've missed you, too."

They talked every day online and frequently over the phone, but that didn't matter. Warren hugged him and then held his hand as they went to wait for his bag. "Did you bring—"

"Yes, I got your books." Silas rolled his eyes. "Text Tal, tell him I'm here and he can tell you his good news."

Warren narrowed his eyes. "What good news?"

Silas grinned. "Text Tal."

"He asked her."

"No, she asked him." Silas bounced. "Three years before the wedding, at least, but that girl is determined. Gave him a ring and everything."

Warren hugged him again. "That's so freaking awesome."

"I know, right? Only thing better is this." He pulled a tattered envelope out of his pocket and handed it to Warren. "Oh, there's my bag." He darted off, leaving Warren to read the letter on his own.

Warren didn't have to. As soon as he saw the letterhead, he knew.

They were going to be together, maybe as early as the summer, and they were going to have such a good life.

The proof was right there, smiling at him.

Prove It

CPSIA information can be obtained at www.ICGtesting.com
Printed in the USA
270008BV00009B/10/P